Ravenous

Jaymie Acosta

About the Author

Jaymie Acosta loves adventure, loves reading, and loves making people laugh. At present, she lives in the isolated mountains of Vermont, but has called places like Florida, Hawaii, New York, and Canada as home.

Life is too short and she wants to experience it all.

Let her take you on an adventure.

www.jaymieacosta.com

jaymie@jaymieacosta.com

Jaymie Acosta

Chapter One

Day seven of my cycle

Cold iron bit into my wrists when I rolled on my side and turned my back toward the door. The insistent knocking drilled into my aching head. I stifled a moan. If I stayed real quiet maybe they'd leave, thinking the motel room was empty. From the searing pain in my abdomen and the weakening demands of my inner demon, I only had a few hours left to live.

The crack of wood splintering replaced the pounding. I jerked at the sharp noise and twisted around. Hanging on the hinges, my door had smashed open. Someone flicked the switch on and the lights burned my sensitive eyes. I tried to shield my face with my hand but the chains holding the manacles around my wrists clanked and held my arm inches from the mattress.

"No." I yelled. "Get out!" My chains rattled as I lunged at them. They snapped me back against the mattress and my head flopped on the pillow as a surge of sexual frustration flooded my system. My demon nature had quieted to a dull roar since yesterday but the scent of males had awoken the beast. It roared inside my head and clawed to retake control of my body. "Yes, stay," it whispered.

Two people strode into the room. Light haloed around them so I couldn't make any details. "Close the door, Cooper." The shorter one knelt by my bed. "You look terrible for a succubus."

I blinked my eyes until I could focus, and cleared my throat. "Get the fuck out." I just wanted to die and take my demon with me.

The young man tilted his head to the side as if confused. Blond with blue eyes the same shade as a tropical sea, he didn't look much older than nineteen. "I'm here to rescue you, sweetheart." He caressed my cheek and all thoughts of saving him stopped on a dime.

I leaned into his touch and purred. "Yes, let me go." My demon fought me for control.

He jumped to his feet and stepped back, his gaze caressing my body as if trying to decide where to start undressing me. "Fuck."

I'd seen human males react to me this way. The hungrier I grew, the more they would want me. Neither of us could control that reaction. My body would pump fuck-me pheromones in the air until it was fed.

The second man came into my view, a little taller than the blond, with tawny hair down to his muscled shoulders. His thread bare t-shirt and faded jeans clung to all the right places. "What's wrong?"

"Look at her body. She's emaciated. Someone left her here to starve." He watched me as I struggled against my chains.

I could only sit in the back of my head and scream in silence. What I called my demon nature was really a survival instinct. It grew more powerful when I got too hungry. I'd find myself humping some schmuck behind a Dumpster if I didn't feed every three days. This was day seven.

I shuddered. This drive to orgasm was what ruined my *life*. All I ever wanted was to be loved. Why could every other creature have it but my kind?

The blond searched the bathroom, the closet and under my bed. "I don't think it's a trap. If it was, they would have set her loose on us by now."

"A trap?" Tawny, gorgeous Cooper retreated to the door. "You said we were here to help her." He readjusted the crotch of his tight jeans. His gaze wandered back to me and he swallowed hard.

"We are, but I wasn't expecting *this*. Her father said she'd run away but this looks more like a kidnapping."

"Well, unchain her and let's go."

The blond grew still and glared at Cooper. Suddenly, he didn't seem nineteen anymore and the power radiating off him sent my supernatural Richter scale off the chart. So, not human, which explained how he knew my father.

Cooper shrank against the door, his gaze pinned to the cheap carpeting. "Sorry."

"Sorry, what?"

"Sorry, master." His voice shook.

"Use your fucking nose and see if you can pick up the scent of whoever chained her to the bed." The master ran a finger along the sole of my foot.

I rolled my hips, inviting him to take off the yoga pants. I wanted his hands on my skin, not teasing my feet. No, no touching, no feeling. I clawed at the demon. I wouldn't lose this time.

Cooper had walked around the room sniffing at random areas. "It's hard to pinpoint scents in motel rooms, Zur-Sin. There's too much traffic, but hers are the freshest and I don't pick up anything else as new."

That name snapped both me and my demon out of our horny trance. Oh, shit. I'd heard of him. If the devil was a rock star, Zur-Sin was his lead guitarist.

"Look at her." There was a touch of awe in Zur-Sin's voice. "Starved and in desperate need of a shower, yet she's got me eager enough to cum in my pants like I was fifteen all over again." He glanced at his erection, then at Cooper's. "You too. Now *that's* power." He pulled out his phone and took a picture of me. "See? I'm even sending proof to Flynn."

"No!" I cried out. Fear of hurting my father somehow trumped my demon for a second and gained control again.

"Oops, too late." He shook his head. "What am I going to do with you, Pia?"

I kicked at Zur-Sin's hand. "Don't touch me." Oh God, yes please. Touch, kiss, lick…

Cooper was searching the drawers. "Flynn paid us to find her. You can't keep her." He hesitated and shot Zur-Sin a quick glance. "Master."

"We found her."

Cooper rubbed his temples. "How did I ever let myself get talked into this? He's going to be so mad." That was the understatement of the year. My father ruled Lake City. He wouldn't get mad. He'd get even, with interest.

Zur-Sin unbuttoned his shirt, revealing a body that equaled his reputation. Oh god, I could eat him up, vomit, and do it all over again.

I turned my head away so he wouldn't see my tears. I was so tired. How much longer could I fight?

He set his shirt on the back of the chair and worked on his pants.

Cooper made a face of disgust. "Are you out of your mind?" He forgot to address his master properly again.

"We have to feed her. If we release her, she'll feed from us anyway and probably everyone in this motel. We can't transport her back to Lake City in this state. Get undressed."

"I can't take her against her will." Cooper actually placed himself between me and his master. "I can't let you do it either." He clenched his fists as if ready to fight.

Zur-Sin glanced at me over Cooper's shoulders and addressed me. "Shifters are so dramatic. The wolves are the worst." He grabbed Cooper by the throat so fast I didn't see his arm move. "We're not raping her. We're feeding her. She's a succubus. That means she needs sex to live, and from the looks of her I think she's on the verge of dying. Flynn won't pay us if we return with a corpse." He set Cooper aside. "Go outside and guard the door. I'll call you if she needs more than what I can give."

Cooper couldn't look at me. I wanted to tell him it was okay. This wasn't the first time a stranger took advantage of my hunger and unfortunately, since they'd found me too soon, it probably wouldn't be the last. He shuffled out of the room.

I turned my attention to Zur-Sin, who was already naked, cock in hand, and scowled. The worst part? My own chains kept me prisoner for him to force feed me.

"Let's get this over with before whoever chained you returns." He pulled my yoga pants down to my chained ankles.

The touch of his hands on my skin crested my hunger to such a painful peak I cried out. Damn demon tried clawing through me. Tears spilled from my eyes. It hurt. No, I wouldn't let her win.

He crawled on top of me. "I promise. I'll kill the bastard who did this, slowly. I will even let you watch if you want." The dirty bastard lifted my shirt and exposed my breasts. He didn't need access to the girls to feed me.

I arched back and tried to knee him in the crotch. "Nobody did this to me." My chains saved his balls since I didn't have enough slack to finish the move.

His eyes went wide as he pinned my legs under him. "What?"

Twisting my body under him, I elbowed him under the chin. The strike jolted my funny bone and I cried out at the sharp pain.

Blood trickled from Zur-Sin's lip. "Fuck." He pinned my upper arms to the bed as well. "Stop it. I'm trying to save you."

"Leave me alone. I don't want to feed." Pushing those words past my demon's control, I was tired of being its slave. It wrecked everything. No one would ever love me if I had to be a slut. Even as I said the words my demon half wrapped my legs around Zur-Sin's hips. Fighting was futile. That's why I'd chained myself to the bed after my fourth day. My demon nature couldn't feed if it couldn't escape the room. I hadn't expected take-out to show up.

"You did this on purpose?" He grew very still and his real age showed again. It weighed upon me, crushing my soul and my will. "You won't die today, Pia." He thrust his hard cock inside me without even checking if I was ready.

I was, though. I'd been ready since my third day in this motel. Days four and five were a blur. I *did* recall gnawing on my wrist to break free on day six. Luckily I didn't have shifter teeth. By this morning my demon side had retreated, resigned to conserve what little energy we had left until the rescue duo crashed in here.

He pumped his hips harder and faster, his breath

11

hitching in my ear.

Somehow I managed to beat the demon. Where had this discipline been a week ago when I had *really* needed it? Things would have been so different.

The burn of his entry set me on fire. The demon struggled against the chains in an attempt to reach Sin's body, to feel his taut muscles slide under his skin as he tried to bring both of us pleasure. The demon had my body but I still controlled my mind. I didn't want this. I didn't want him. I was done being a parasite. I was done breaking hearts. Especially my own.

Zur-Sin shuddered and grew still upon me while out of breath. Leaning up on his elbow, he assessed my face. "You still look starved. Didn't that do anything?"

I turned my face away and stared at the same spot on the wall I'd been watching for days.

"Hey." He tucked his finger under my chin and turned my face toward him. "What did I do wrong?"

I clenched my teeth so the demon wouldn't speak in my voice.

He rolled off me and pulled his phone out of his pocket from the pants on the floor. "I can't imagine a more awkward conversation than having to ask your daddy how to fuck you."

I narrowed my gaze. He wouldn't dare.

He hit a button and I heard the number dial.

"Stop it!" I sprang against my restraints to knock the phone from his hand, only to be snapped back on the bed. The worn abrasions on my wrists began to bleed once more and I screamed mindlessly.

Zur-Sin's gaze riveted to the blood leaking from my injuries, then he hung up. "Tell me how to feed you." The command in his voice came with a practiced ease of someone who expected everyone to obey.

"*I'm* the one who has to orgasm, dumbass."

"What did you call me?" The genuine shock on his face would have made me laugh a few weeks ago. Now, it just made me tired. His eyes flashed from baby blue to soulless black. I'd just assumed he was Cooper's dominant pack mate. Nope. He stretched his jaw open while his fangs extended. That explained the power surge I'd felt before.

Vampire.

He sat on the edge of my bed and licked the drips of blood from my wrists. He smacked his lips. "Lacks any flavor. You've really depleted yourself. Cooper!" He rose as the shifter hurried inside and he pointed at me. "She needs an orgasm to feed." He slapped Cooper on the back. "Don't let her down." The vampire went into the bathroom. "Don't take all night, either. We've got a long drive ahead of us."

Chapter Two

Cooper had his hands so deep in his front pockets it looked as if they'd been swallowed. He stared at the closed bathroom door until finally, his gaze moved to me. "Why couldn't he feed you?"

"He didn't know the rules."

The shifter heaved a big sigh. "Where are the keys to the restraints?"

I shook my head as if I hadn't a clue.

"I'm a shifter, if you haven't guessed. We have pretty good hearing so I know you chained yourself." He turned a slow circle and sniffed.

My demon was close to the surface, as if we shared the same space. I tracked Cooper as he moved slowly around the room.

"I'm the best hunter in my pack. Zur-Sin had me follow your scent all over the place trying to find you." He looked under the dresser. "Ever drive with your head out the window with a vampire behind the wheel of a sports car? When a bug hits you at that speed it could knock your eye out."

I chuckled then clamped my mouth shut.

Cooper circled toward me. "You couldn't have tossed it far, since you're chained up." His gaze moved toward the edge of the mattress where it met the wall, next to my hand. He bent to look under the bed. I heard some scrambling as he moved under me, until he came up with the key dangling in his hand. "Ta-da. I knew you couldn't have thrown with your wrists restrained."

"I had aimed for the trashcan." It was five feet to his left.

He chuckled and hurried to the bedside. "Sure you were."

"Don't do it, Cooper. I'll hurt you."

"I'm a werewolf. I think I can handle a little thing like you." He started with my ankles. After he undid the manacle, he rubbed the circulation back into my raw skin. "How long have you been here?"

I kicked him in the kidney. "Don't be nice to me."

He clutched his side and grinned even wider. "Okay." Yet, he went to work on the other ankle, wrestling my leg under his arm until he got it unlocked. He wiped the sweat off his brow. "So you're stronger than you look. Maybe someone should clue me in as to what's going on? Your dad said you'd gone missing. He didn't know if you'd run away from college or if someone had kidnapped you. The human police weren't any help so he hired…" He pointed his thumb at the bathroom. "Who had my alpha force me into this." He hesitated by the bed. "What will happen if I free you?"

"I'll tear your clothes off and most likely fuck you to death."

15

He stared and his Adam's apple moved as he swallowed.

"Go home, Cooper." I used the same tone of command Zur-Sin had.

Cooper sat down by my head and ran his fingers through my matted curls. They got tangled and he struggled to get free. "I mean if your goal is dying, you could just call Zur-Sin a dumbass again."

The click of a lock on my wrist had me twisting toward him. "Are you crazy? What do you think will happen afterwards when I'm standing over your dead body? Why would you think I could live with that?" His scent invaded my senses. I'd tamped down the demon once but I didn't have strength left. "Get away," I whispered. My voice cracked with desperation.

"Nah." He reached over me to undo my other manacle. "I don't mind feeding you. I just won't do it while you're chained to a bed. That might be his kink, but it isn't mine. Neither of us will die. Zur-Sin will make sure of that, right?" He shouted the last word toward the bathroom.

"You haven't any idea what I've done. I'm a terrible person." I tried to dash away.

He paused to regard me. "Well, I'd say a werewolf and a vampire are the worst people to judge others on their sins." He undid the last lock. "Where do you want to—?"

The demon must have been waiting. As soon as the lock clicked open, it shoved me so far back in my hindbrain that I barely realized I had Cooper pinned on the carpet. I'd straddled him and had his t-shirt torn open.

Golden wolf eyes met mine. It was like he pierced my soul and soothed me into the backseat, letting the demon drive the bus. His rough hands fondled my breasts as I struggled with his jeans.

A broken nail and a demonic wail later, I had it open and snaked my hand to caress his cock. My heart raced. No matter how I tried to control my demon, it would hurt Cooper. Every time I got hold of my control, it just wiggled as if covered in butter, and the demon smacked me back.

He pulled my shirt over my head and yanked my yoga pants off the rest of the way.

My demon guided Cooper inside and started riding him greedily, but I had to reach orgasm to feed. What had the mailman done after he left my home? I struggled against the pleasure Cooper was giving me. Would Frank tell his wife? I'd not only fucked up my life and Pierre's. I'd hurt an innocent couple's life as well. I gripped the raw pain. I wouldn't feed. The demon could do what it wanted with my body but we would starve. I'd kill that bitch for what's she'd done.

Cooper sat up and cradled my face, staring into my eyes. "Pia," he whispered my name.

Oh god.

He leaned forward, pressing the gentlest of kisses on my lips while letting me grind our hips together.

Oh no.

He repeated my name but this time it came with less control and a more passionate growl.

Oh yes.

I gripped his strong shoulders, digging my ragged nails into his skin, and kissed him back. Orgasm struck me like a linebacker from behind, making me arch my spine so far back I couldn't believe it hadn't cracked. Stars spun in my vision as my screams faded. I gulped air as my lung burned for oxygen. The energy created from our coupling curled into my lower abdomen, easing the sharp empty ache. Cooper tasted of the hunt and full moon. I groaned and savored my first meal in days, but I needed seconds.

He melted to the floor. "Wow." Then his eyes rolled back into his head.

I shook his shoulder. "Cooper?"

He didn't respond.

"Cooper?" An edge of panic crept into my voice.

Zur-Sin was suddenly next to me, checking the shifter's pulse. He had his pants on. "He's alive." He then checked my face and eyes. "You don't look better."

I clutched my stomach. "I'm still hungry."

"I bet you are." He nudged me off the shifter and scooped up Cooper. "Let me settle him, then we'll take care of you."

On my knees, I dry heaved while Sin tucked the shifter on the motel room's couch. That was sneaky of Cooper to kiss me. I was such a sucker for romantic gestures, even the corny ones. I was starved on more than just the metaphysical demonic level. Normally a feed like what Cooper had just given me would fill me for three days. I wouldn't have left him unconscious, but my demon pulled everything he had to give me without killing him. Thank goodness. I preferred Cooper alive.

Zur-Sin took me by the hand, leading me to the bathroom. "Let's clean you." He turned on the shower and shoved me in the stall.

Ice-cold water poured over my head. I shrieked and tried to jump out but every time I tried to escape, he just shoved me back in with his supernatural strength and speed. I sputtered when he poured cheap motel shampoo on my tangled curls and scrubbed. The water grew warmer.

"How do you manage this mess?" He tried to pull his fingers through my hair.

"Ow, ow, ow." I slapped his hands. "Stop that. I need conditioner for the tangles." I'd been in bed for seven days. That tends to make a rat's nest on the back of someone's head.

He read the small bottle. "Says two-in-one shampoo/conditioner."

"It's not strong enough for my kind of hair. Just leave it alone." The water had grown much hotter and steamed the bathroom now. I'd inherited my father's curls, so regular hair products couldn't control the crazy.

Zur-Sin slipped out of his pants and squeezed

under the shower with me and he brought soap. With slow strokes, he ran it over my skin.

I couldn't breathe. I stood with my back to the cool tiles and watched his long-fingered hand move over my breasts. The hunger rampaged through my body. It took all my will power not to jump him like I'd done Cooper.

He circled my nipples, making them rigid until they throbbed, then he moved his hands lower. "I was too impatient before." His expression still remained serious. "Can't remember the last time I wanted someone so badly."

"It's the demon part of me. When I'm hungry enough I send out *fuck-me* pheromones."

He smirked and leaned his arm against the wall by my head until we were kissing-close. His lips brushed mine as he spoke. "Then fuck me, Pia."

A shiver ran over my spine. The claws of hunger still had a hold on me. Without chains to hold me back, I didn't have the power to stop myself. Running my fingers through his hair, I gazed into his eyes that had returned to a beautiful blue. How could someone with a reputation of being so evil look so innocent?

With a sinking heart, I realized the demon had won. Again. How did my mothers and sisters do this every three days without hating themselves?

He pulled away. "Does it matter how you orgasm?"

"Someone other than me has to give me one.

Male, female doesn't matter. Masturbation won't work."

A slow smile curled his lips before he knelt in front of me. "I think I can manage that."

My heart skipped a beat when his hands pressed between my thighs to spread my legs.

"Don't tell me you're shy." He grinned wide enough to expose his sharp fangs. They grew under my watchful eyes. "Let me show a trick I know."

The last adjective I would have used to describe me was shy, but I'd only had one lover over the last six months and I'd loved him so much. It felt odd having another man touch me so intimately now that the demon part of my soul had loosened the reins on my libido. At his urging, I slid my legs apart.

He went so far as to guide my left leg over his shoulder. "Like that. Now brace your hands on my shoulders. We don't want you to slip."

I did as he ordered, as if I moved within a dream. My limbs trembled with weakness. I wasn't in any shape for any acrobatics.

Leaning forward, he kissed my lower abdomen as his finger slipped inside me. He slid in and out of me with a slow rhythm that matched his wandering kisses.

A small moan escaped my lips. My gaze was trapped by what he was doing. Most of my experiences came from humans. My parents didn't like me feeding from bars that catered to the paranormal community. They thought I was too young. My race was long lived and being

21

nineteen meant my parents still hovered over every move I made. Then they wondered why I'd decided to go to college outside Lake City.

Zur-Sin slid another finger inside of me, increasing the pace. He ran his fangs over my groin until they rested on my pulse point.

A wave of dizziness washed over me and I leaned my head against the cool tile. I'd never been with a vampire, let alone been food for one. *I* was usually the predator in the bed. An ache inside my heart grew more intense. It had been there all along but I'd gotten so used to the dull roar that I'd almost forgotten it existed. Tears slid unchecked down my cheeks, mixing in with the water from the shower. Nothing more pitiful than a crying succubus during sex and I didn't want a vampire's pity, because who better to understand me than another parasite.

He rolled my clitoris between his fingers with just enough pressure bordering on pain.

I hissed at the sudden jolt of pleasure that sizzled away my dark emotions. It jerked my attention back to the vampire with the crystal blue gaze.

"I don't know where you went mentally but I want you to stay here with me." He eased his pinch, replacing with gentle rubbing. He lowered his mouth to my pulse point and struck. The sharp pain made me gasp but Zur-Sin's talented fingers stroked all my good spots at the same time. Both sensations of pain and pleasure tangled in a rush that left me breathless. I dug my nails into his shoulders.

The pain of his bite lessened, replaced by his soft, moist mouth as he fed. Warmth spread over my body from the inside out and had nothing to do with the shower. The knots in my shoulders relaxed and I took a deep breath, the first in over a week. I leaned into Zur-Sin's hold, letting him support my weight and allowing the bliss to sweep away the emptiness in my heart.

Pressure built in my lower abdomen, a familiar friend. I rocked my hips in time to his fingers as his sucking grew stronger, harder. Inarticulate noise fell from my lips as he ground against my bud with an expert's skill. I closed my eyes as the orgasm struck me almost blind.

Zur-Sin's flavor slammed over my senses, full of spicy tingling power that left my insides raw and craving for more. I'd never experienced anything like this before. Humans had flavors as well but they were vanilla to his tutti-frutti.

My eyelids finally fluttered open. "Wow."

He paused in licking his bite mark closed and I could sense his smug smile against my skin. "You liked that?"

I slid down the wall onto his lap. "Finger licking good."

He threw back his head and laughed. "I haven't been food for someone else in a very, very long time."

"This is my first time being food as well." I ran my fingertips over his healing bite mark. I tilted my head and assessed his young face. "You don't even look tired. I fed just as hard on Cooper and he passed out."

Zur-Sin kissed the tip of my nose. "How long have you been starving yourself?"

Our gazes met and stuck. I couldn't pull away from his intense magnetism. Why did he want to know? I blinked and jerked from his touch. "I—I think it's time for you to go."

His grin faded and he rose with me in his arms. With his elbow, he shut off the shower. "I agree." He set me on my feet and proceeded to towel dry me. He fingered the autumn-colored curls I'd inherited from my father. "The sun will be close to rising by the time we get to Lake City, so we'll finish feeding you when we get home."

I turned away from the vampire's searching stare. "I'm not allowed to feed at home. Dad's rule." The last people I wanted to see were my parents. "I won't go there."

"Fine, not your home. My home. Your family can't care for you in this state anyways. Not unless they keep men in their basement for snacks. I spoke with your father while you were feeding off Cooper. He's very…distraught."

A stab of concern woke me from the post feeding haze. "You really sent him that picture?"

"Of course. He needs to know what I'm dealing with."

"You're a jerk."

"I'm much, much worse than that." He gripped

my chin and yanked my face closer to his. "Your father is paying me very well to save your pretty ass, so I will force feed you until you're plump." Yanking the blanket off the bed, he wrapped me in it.

"What about my clothes?"

"Leave them. We'll get you something clean." He dressed then scooped inert Cooper into his arms, carrying the shifter outside. "Follow me."

I glanced at the chains on the bed. Death had seemed like my only escape a week ago. I came really close to achieving my goal. I fingered the blood-stained manacle. Really close…

If I went with Zur-Sin, it meant I chose to live. That meant no more starving and I'd have to make an effort to heal. Could I forgive myself for destroying so many people's happiness? I might be able to discover a way, but I wasn't sure my family could. We were of the succubus/incubus charm of Lake City. We didn't have many rules but if you broke the ones we did have, there wasn't any forgiveness. Sleeping with a married person would get me shunned.

I'd rather have no contact with my family. Their rejection would destroy what was left of my heart.

Zur-Sin popped his head back through the threshold. "Pia," he said my name sharply. "That wasn't a request."

On wobbly legs, I shuffled after him.

Chapter Three

I slid low in the passenger seat of Zur-Sin's black SUV and watched the traffic we passed at sonic speed. "You'll get pulled over driving this fast." The vampire wouldn't let me play the radio and left me to stew in uncomfortable silence as we returned to Lake City. Silence being a figurative state. Cooper snored like a coffee grinder while sprawled in the backseat. "Maybe we should roll him over so he doesn't swallow his tongue."

The vampire frowned but reached over with one hand and carelessly tugged Cooper onto his side. "There." He seemed grumpy ever since we'd left the shower.

I pulled the blanket around my shoulders even tighter. If he was pissed at me then he needed to take a ticket. Between my family, ex-boyfriend, and my postman's family, it felt like most of the world hated me. If I hadn't been born then everyone could be happy again.

"Tell me." Zur-Sin weaved between two eighteen-wheelers, passing them with an inch to spare.

With my heart in my throat, I pried my fingers from the chicken bar. "You do realize I'm young enough to still die from a car accident."

"*Now* you want to live." He grinned. The bastard had done that on purpose. "Just wanted to make sure."

"There's a difference between starving and being road kill." I twisted in my seat to face his profile. "I know your name, but not how you're connected to my father."

"I'm wounded." His words dripped with sarcasm. "I used to be your father's lieutenant. The one he doesn't talk about."

Oh, that one. My father ruled Lake City's paranormal community. The humans didn't know of our existence but there were a lot of us around. Blending in helped. My people had given up our wings and demonic powers to appear more human ages ago. It made hunting so much easier. Zur-Sin was the person my father used to do the nasty things that were sometimes required, like hunting down his missing youngest daughter.

"Wait, 'used to be'?"

His expression changed slightly but he seemed like a cat who'd just stolen a whole gallon of cream. "Your father loves you very much. When you stopped answering your phone, he got in touch with that human you had shacked up with. The little turd told your dad that you'd moved out but not why, so I was sent to ask instead." He shook his head. "Nasty business that."

My heart seized. That little turd was the love of my life. I grabbed Zur-Sin's arm. It hurt to breathe. "What did you do to Pierre?"

"Nothing physical. Human minds are very weak. I had a snack and pulled the answers from his mind. Interesting story. I think your father was willing to part with everything for your safe return."

27

A lump formed in my throat. I bit the inside of my hot cheeks to keep from uttering a sound. I knew my daddy loved me. The damn bloodsucker didn't need to grind it in. The shame I'd bring to my family had driven me to run. I couldn't bear to see the disappointment on their faces. "Did you tell him?" My voice cracked.

He chuckled. "Your people have such strange morals."

"Did you tell him?" I shouted it this time and hit the dash with my fist.

He gave me an icy stare. "No."

"What did he give you to find me?" The house? His bank account? Never my mothers or sisters. He'd never hurt any of us.

"Half his power. I'll be co-ruling Lake City."

"Only half? How generous of you." It was worse than I'd hoped. My father and mothers had worked so hard to bring the different communities together in Lake. Our co-existence was beneficial to everyone. "Why not the whole thing?"

"The sun. I can't do anything during the day. Your father handles the businesses and the politics very well. No point in my destroying that. The night, though. There's a lot your father has forbade me to do." He flashed me a fanged grin. "Not anymore. I think I'll start with my own nightclub."

I sat very still. My father had given up half his power so Zur-Sin could return me, his useless dropout daughter. I was so broken. I didn't think they made a glue strong enough to put me back together again. "I wish you'd never found me."

He stared at the interstate, one hand on the steering wheel. Nothing he said would make me feel better and it seemed he knew.

Pierre could tell Zur-Sin only half the story. My human boyfriend didn't know about succubi or any other creatures that bumped in the night. All he knew was that he'd caught me cheating on him. He wouldn't ever understand how starved I'd been and how my demon nature had finally gained control of me, setting me to feed on the first male I came across.

My stomach rolled with nausea.

"You look like a vampire who's been buried alive for half a year. I don't think that happens in seven days to a succubus."

"I did something stupid." I pulled my knees up to my chest and wrapped my arms around them, unable to look at anyone. Not even the jackass bloodsucker who'd seen me at my worst. "I fell in love." Most of my people treated love like a disease or a tool to get what they wanted. A succubus in love was vulnerable unless the person loved her back enough to let her feed properly and freely. Open relationships existed, but they were hard won unless you were from my kind. We *had* to have open marriages.

Incubi could only feed from succubi and one wasn't enough to feed him for long. For them to collect enough of us to feed from, incubi had discovered it was easier to offer succubi security and money in exchange for exclusive feeding rights, also known as marriage in my culture. The more powerful the incubi, the more wives he had. Love didn't figure into the equation, except with my parents. They were considered eccentric. My three mothers and my one father loved each other fiercely. How could they expect me to want something different?

"I only fed from Pierre for the last six months."

He nodded. "If I fed from only one human for six months, that human would be dead. How is Pierre alive?"

"I didn't take much. Just enough to stay alive."

"That's stupid."

"Thank you."

"Your father said you'd have to feed more frequently until you're better. Do you know how much?"

I shrugged. "I never let it get this bad before and don't know anyone who has. Succubi aren't known for their restraint."

"When we see your family tomorrow night we can figure that out."

"I don't want to see them," I whispered.

"Pia…"

I undid my seat belt and slid closer to him, leaning my forehead on his shoulder. "Please." Zur-Sin was a top of the class jerk so I didn't know why I bothered except I thought he had an itty-bitty soft spot for me. "Don't make me go. I'll agree to anything but that. You can take pictures of me that I'm well, as proof. Whatever, to keep them away."

He didn't say anything at first. We just drove for a few minutes with me clinging to his arm. "Anything?"

I swallowed hard. "Yes."

"I'm not prone to letting strangers into my nest." He tapped his finger on the steering wheel as if thinking hard. "They're my family, you understand. And you're out of control."

"Okay." I sounded so meek. When had that happened? The succubus I'd been, who had left for college a year ago, had been assertive and confident. She seemed like a faded memory now.

"I'll set you up in one of my safe houses and send somebody over to feed you. Your father can pick you up in the morning."

Nausea rolled in my stomach. "I don't like feeding from strangers." What would I say to my dad? *Hey, I did exactly what you warned me not to do and you were right. I suck.*

"You fed from me and Cooper."

"I was starved enough. I'm more sentient now." That seemed like the right word. When my demon took over it was like another being, but really, the demon was me as well. Just like a shifter when he went wolf. We were both animalistic and running on instinct.

I returned to my side of the vehicle and pulled down the sunshade to look at myself in the mirror. Sin was right. I looked terrible with eyes that were sunken and dark, pale and dull skin; even my crazy curls had less spring to them. This after *two* feedings. What had I looked like when they came into the room?

Zur-Sin chuckled. "I don't run a catering service for succubus. You'll have to make do with what I send."

"If I'm not attracted to them, I won't orgasm."

He growled.

"Threatening me won't make me orgasm either." I closed the sunshade, unable to look at myself anymore. Returning to Lake City was a mistake. If I was going to try to live with what I'd done, then facing my family before I was ready would flip my switch to self-destruct again. They'd be so disappointed with me. One step at a time.

"It's not like I have a menu, Pia. What do you suggest?"

"Drop me off at a bar. I'll shop around. You won't have to worry about me anymore." How hard could it be to steal a car? Maybe I could find someone to give me one. My sister Rose did it all the time, though she didn't look like the walking dead. I could drive north or buy a plane ticket to a tropical island. My dad shouldn't have cut off my credit cards yet.

One thing was for sure. I wouldn't see my family tomorrow. That was that.

Zur-Sin side-eyed me. "A bar? Dressed in just a blanket?"

I glanced down. Well, shit. A traitorous tear spilled over my cheek and swiped it away.

"I forbid you to do that." The vampire frowned and accelerated the car as if he could race my tears to Lake City.

"I don't want to wait in some h-hotel room like some wh-whore waiting for tricks." I stared out the window trying to hide my face. "You should have left me alone." The last part I had whispered so low it surprised me even his vampire hearing had caught it.

"Fuck." He strangled the steering wheel. "You'll come to the nest. Only for tonight and you *will* have to feed again. No more tears." He mumbled something in a language I didn't know, but it sounded close enough to swearing.

"Thank you, Sin. Is it all right if I call you just Sin?"

"No."

"Zur-Sin is an odd name. Where is it from?"

"Babylon."

I'd been right. He was old. "Does it mean anything?"

"Google it."

He took an exit that led to the forested suburbs where most of Lake City's wolf pack lived. Sin pulled up to a remote cabin and carried Cooper inside, leaving me in the SUV. Not long after, he returned and drove us to the industrial section of the city to an old abandoned garage. He pulled inside the building and parked the SUV among a

33

few other more expensive-looking vehicles and motorcycles. "Home sweet home." He turned off the SUV and exited, leaving me to scramble and follow.

Under my bare feet, the cement felt cool. Little rocks stabbed at my soles. I did my best to wrap the blanket around my skeletal body, trying to hide the important bits.

Sin was already at a metallic door and it swung open on its own. The thing was very thick. Inside the threshold was what I could only describe as a security stop, since three armed males greeted us. "Boys, this is Pia. She's staying for the night."

Chapter Four

I blinked in the bright lights of the security room. Television screens were mounted on the walls with multiple camera feeds from what appeared to be outside and inside the nest. I steeled my spine at the military cut of Sin's home. From the pictures reflected on the screens, everything seemed made of a minimalist's dream. I couldn't picture a more opposite place from the home I grew up in.

The guards eyed me with a combination of curiosity, distaste, and lust. I wasn't used to the distaste part but I remembered my disheveled appearance in the SUV's mirror. I looked like I'd been ridden hard and long. One of them grabbed my hand and assessed the manacle damage around my wrist. He shook his head and let me go without comment.

Sin punched a long series of numbers into a pad by another steel door. It slid into the wall like something from a science fiction film. As soon as I followed through it snapped shut, almost catching the tail end of my blanket.

"This is like Fort Knox. Paranoid much?" We stood in what I could only call a grand living room with plenty of couches in different shades of gray. It obviously was created for social events but was completely empty.

"We're vulnerable during the day. Security is the number one thing vampires crave." He paused halfway across the room and I almost ran into his back. "This is the largest vampire nest in the northeast. Do you know why?"

My mouth hung open as I tried to kick start my brain. "Uh…because you give them security?"

He gave me a small smile and I half expected him to pat me on the head like a good dog. "Yes. I protect what's mine and in return they give me loyalty."

"What happens if they're disloyal?"

"Depends." He shrugged. "They get a private session with me in the dungeons and either they die or they live." When Sin said the word *dungeon* I didn't think he meant the kind used in the local BDSM club, Cleaver, that catered to the paranormal community. Something as old as him wouldn't understand the niceties of this age like safe words. He traced my face with a fingertip. "Just be a good girl, Pia. It's not that hard." Obviously, he knew nothing about me.

"Sure. Do I get clothes?" I let the blanket fall.

His gaze dropped to my body almost as fast as the blanket had fallen off. "We'll find you something. Follow me." He led me deeper into the building.

I rewrapped the blanket around me and hurried. We passed a few people, some working at computers, others playing games. One was working on the plumbing in the wall. Nobody bowed or scraped to Sin but they all hesitated as he passed, watching him from the corners of their eyes.

He waited for me by an elevator when his cell phone rang. He answered it. "Flynn."

I stopped mid-step. That was my dad. I shook my head.

"Yes, she's here." He paused. "She doesn't want to talk to you." He rolled his eyes. "I'm not a nurse maid. She's out tomorrow. If she won't go home with you then that's not my problem. I brought her back to Lake City. It's up to you to keep her here."

I could hear my father's voice grow louder and more threatening. Many races took mine for granted, thinking us powerless sex mongers, but they all fell prey to us when we wanted. My father had proven this. He'd taken Lake City by storm all by himself and brought order to it so his daughters would have a safe place to grow up. I loved him so hard.

Zur-Sin's face grew serious. "That wasn't part of the deal." His narrow gaze daggered me. "I experienced Pia's power first hand."

I took a step back. I didn't like the calculating look in Sin's eyes.

"What are you offering?" He reached out and twirled one of my curls around his finger. "I want a blood contract. Something that's binding. We can knock out the details tomorrow." *He* hung up on my *father* and gave me a smug smile. "Daddy doesn't trust you."

"What did you do?" I yanked away from his touch

and ignored the sharp pain from my pulled hair.

His eyes went wide and innocent. "*I* didn't do anything." He held out his hands like he hadn't just coerced my father into another deal. "Seems like your father is worried about your feeding habits. That's not *my* fault."

"What deal did you agree to?" I crossed my arms.

"That depends on you. Do you want to go back to your family or stay with me?"

"That's like asking me if I want to stab myself in the left eye or the right. The answer's neither."

"You act like you have a choice. How far do you think you can run before Daddy sends me after you again? And how much are you willing to let him lose in the process?"

"You're a top class jerk."

He raised an eyebrow as if waiting for my answer.

"Here."

"As long as you live in my nest you belong to me. You sleep with who I tell you to without question. You do as you're told. That's the only way I'll agree to this."

I leaned toward him. "My dad's paying you to take care of me. Why should I listen to you?"

He gripped my chin and pulled up until we were breathing each other's air. "Because I don't need you. My life would be easier without having a spoiled princess to watch over." He dropped me.

I caught my balance and glanced over my shoulder at the metal door exiting outside. This was it. Once I agreed to Sin's demands I'd be cutting off my family for good. Sure, I had left them when I'd gone to college but there had been visits and phone calls. From now on Pia Marie Blyton would vanish and only Pia would exist.

I nodded. He'd won. I rather give up my freedom. It's what I deserved anyway.

He passed a key card over a sensor to activate the elevator. According to the numbers on the control panel inside the elevator, we were on the top floor. We dropped halfway to level ten and exited into a more crowded area. "It's getting close to sunrise, so most of my people have returned." He pointed across the room. "The kitchen is well stocked. I expect you to make your own meals or seduce one of the humans who live here to do it for you." Grabbing my hand, he pulled me through the crowded room.

I struggled to get free but Sin didn't seem to notice. People brushed against me on each side. I moaned and clutched my lower abdomen. All there was between me and them was this cheap blanket. I only had to drop it. Was Sin trying to set off an orgy?

We stood in a recreation room with the biggest flat screen TV I'd ever seen. A soccer game was on and the space was standing-room only.

I caught my hand reaching out to caress the closest person to me. *Damn it. Pull it together, Pia.* I tucked my hands under my armpits.

39

Sin leaned toward a male. "Who's winning?"

"Rio."

"Fuck." Sin grimaced.

"For once you might owe me money." The male spoke absently, his gaze riveted on the television until he saw me. His attention suddenly swung my way. "Who's this?"

"Rat, this is Pia. My new succubus pet. She needs quarters."

I tried to pretend I wasn't just wearing a blanket. "Nice to meet you." The crush of people around me flared my hunger to critical mass. Touch could do that. I was seconds from jumping anyone. Male, female, sheep…

Rat's gaze wandered over me. "Yeah." Then he turned his back and tugged a huge set of keys off his belt. He went through them until he found the one he wanted and took it off, handing it to me. "Right next to mine, just in case you need a midnight snack."

I snatched it away from him and fled the room. Once by the elevators, I stared at the key. I hoped it locked from the inside as well or that Rat didn't have a master key on that ring. I leaned my forehead against the cool metal of the elevator and panted.

Sin loomed over me. "What's wrong?"

"Nothing, I'm tired." And still hungry but not starved enough to lose complete control and jump the closest person. That was my problem. I wasn't amoral enough to be a succubus. My sisters would have taken Rat's open invitation with a satisfied smile. I, on the other hand, didn't like the way Rat's gaze oozed over my flesh. "I'd like to shower."

"You just did."

I flinched. Neither of us said anything more.

He looked at the room number on the key. "He won't touch you without my permission and I won't give it unless you make me." The threat hung in the air between us. I was his pet. His to punish, to feed, to clothe and whatever else. *Be a good girl, Pia.* What he hadn't said was *or I'll feed you to low-life scum who want nothing more than your body.*

I nodded, not trusting my mouth.

"Gigi," he called to someone farther down the hall.

A small female came hurrying to Sin's side. She kept her eyes downcast and all but huddled against him. Not in fear of him—she seemed more afraid of me.

"You both look the same size. Can you lend Pia something to wear?" He fixed his gaze on me. "I'll get your family to send some of your clothes here tomorrow."

He handed Gigi my key. "Show her where this room is and tell her about the rules."

She nodded and with hesitant fingers gestured for me to follow.

Sin returned to the room where the crowd cheered.

Following Gigi along the long corridor, I passed many used rooms. "I didn't realize there were so many

41

vampires."

"There aren't. The upper floors are mostly for humans." She kept her gaze down and moved fast through the crowded hall. Thank goodness.

I had to shove and push to keep up with her. "Slow down, Gigi." I almost lost the fucking blanket when someone stepped on it. I gave it a hard yank, freeing it from the person's foot.

She slowed to a stop and allowed me to catch up before showing me inside her room. It was very…pink. In the corner stood a wardrobe that she opened. "Take what you want."

Gigi was blond and petite. She had an invisible bruised look to her. My succubus senses were tingling and I didn't mean the sexual ones. For some reason I could sense a supernatural person's power. Sin's power gonged close to a holy-shit scale where Gigi barely registered at all, but it also meant she wasn't human.

If she was a vampire and just recently fed, she could pull off the flushed look. I didn't get a predator vibe from her. She seemed more like prey. I scanned her wardrobe and picked out a pretty green dress with a flared skirt, but her feet were bigger than mine so none of the shoes fit.

"I have flip-flops or slippers. Those don't need to fit that well. It should do for the night." She held up my choices, still not meeting my gaze.

"Flip-flops." I ran my finger under her chin and lifted so we could see eye to eye. "I don't bite, Gigi." I raised my eyebrow. "Do you?"

She grinned. Not because she found me hilarious but to show she didn't have fangs. "You smell like pack."

"I do?" I dropped my hand. "I—I snuggled a wolf shifter today." Part of me cringed at what I said. Snuggling didn't come anywhere close to what I'd done to poor Cooper but Gigi just seemed so—so sweet, I was tripping over my tongue not to offend her.

Her gaze still remained wary. "But you're not one?"

"No, I'm a succubus." I held out my hand. "Pia."

"I'm a wolf shifter." She shook it gently but fast. "I don't like pack." But apparently vampires were okay for her, and for me, so we had a little common ground to work with.

"Why are you living on the human floor?"

"I'm not afraid of them. They really can't harm me. Your room is on the bottom floor, right in the middle of the oldest of the master's vampires."

"Oh, well that sucks." I winked at her. "Pun intended."

She blinked at me as if I was short a few marbles. "Let me show you." This time she didn't race away, leading me to the elevator again. "There are stair cases at the end of each side of the corridors if you'd rather climb."

"When you say 'master,' do you mean Sin?"

Her eyes went wide. "Zur-Sin." She corrected.

"He's *our* master."

I shook my head. "He's my owner, but no one masters me. Not even myself." The elevator doors opened.

She took me to the lowest level. The area was more elegant and less industrial. The lights held a softer tone with less neon. As we strode down the corridors, I noted the rooms seemed much larger. Another elevator stood next to the one we had taken. "Where does the other one go?"

"To the master's private apartment. You need a key to make it run." She stopped in front of a door and unlocked it. "This is your room."

A moan echoed in this quieter part of the nest. Someone was having a good time at least. I leaned to the side to get a better look at my neighbors.

"It's coming from the feeding room." Her eyes grew haunted and she pointed at the end of the hall. "I better go." She almost ran back to the elevator.

I glanced at my room. Bed, closet, desk, whatever. It was a place to sleep. I took note of a shared bathroom across the hall equipped with a few shower stalls and surprisingly a few hot tubs. My bedroom door did lock from the inside with a dead bolt, but I'd assume the lock wouldn't stop a vampire from kicking the whole doorframe down.

Sitting on the edge of my bed, I tried to ignore the sounds traveling from the feeding room. The moans were growing louder and less controlled. Those were not feeding noises. Those were having great sex noises. I stuck my fingers in my ears.

Sin said he would tell me who to feed from, but if he didn't give me a menu soon I'd be going buffet crazy on those fuckers down the hall.

Chapter Five

Someone shook me. I'd curled into a ball on my bed, facing the wall, with my fingers in my ears and humming to myself. Sitting up, I faced the vampire.

"What are you doing?" he asked.

A woman's orgasmic scream echoed down the hall. I pointed in that direction. "How was this supposed to be a good idea, Sin?"

His eyebrows furrowed. "Zur-Sin."

I sat on the edge of my bed, my shoulders slumping in defeat. "I still need to feed." The prospect of jumping some stranger's cock left a bad taste in my mouth. When I'd first started feeding three years ago, one-night stands had been exciting. I'd go out with my sisters and hunt. It was fun. Then I discovered that a lot of males didn't like being cast aside and that I preferred the sweeter varieties of men rather than those who wanted to just bump hips. Those relationships spiraled out of control from there.

Control.

That was the key. I didn't have any. Knowing what I had to do and actually doing it was not working for me. I *should* hunt humans. Use them, discard them, repeat as necessary. Yet as soon as I'd met one who was super nice to me, I fell so hard, so fast I had whiplash.

"Pia!" Sin knelt in front of me, holding my trembling shoulders. "We'll go down to the feeding room and see who's there." He helped me to my feet. "You can choose who you want."

I rested my hand on his chest. "You choose for me." Picking my own meals had proven disastrous. Maybe if I let a jerk like Sin make the decisions, I'd be better at living with my demon nature. My fingers curled, gripping his shirt. "And don't leave me." I hiccupped the last word. Sin could mend my body, but who would fix the really broken parts inside? If I swept my soul free of debris, would there be anything left?

"Come on. The sun is rising so only my older vampires will still be moving around. That might be a good thing." He pried my fingers off his shirt and guided me toward the feeding room. "They'll be curious about you and they have more patience than the younger ones. Most of the time."

For every one of Sin's strides, I had to take two almost running steps. He didn't leave me a choice since he clutched my hand. Ever since he barged into my motel room he hadn't given me *any* choices. He'd made me feed from him and Cooper, two males I'd never met before today, and I still managed to breathe. This was a good thing, I think. A pattern I could manage and live with. I was such a massive fuck-up because I'd been following my heart. What I needed was to ignore my instincts to care about my lovers and just do as Sin told me. Let him have

47

control since he seemed more competent. And ruthless.

Standing in the threshold of the feeding room, I gazed wide-eyed. I didn't know what I was expecting, but not a scene that should have fit in an incubus' den. Large cushions of varying shades of earth tones were piled in the center of the room where all the action was taking place.

I rose to tiptoe and whispered in Sin's ear, "I didn't know vampires did orgies."

He snorted. "Do you think your people have exclusive rights?" He pulled me inside to one of the love seats placed as if for audiences. Nice touch. "Let's watch and see who's here." Leaning his chin on his palm, he observed the bodies in the dim light.

"Are there more rooms like this?" I kicked off my flip-flops and squished my toes into the plush carpet. It must be a bitch to clean this room.

"Not really." He sighed. "Most of my nest is more private about their leisure."

I watched a female vampire feeding from a human male's neck. His mouth hung open as if caught in bliss. "So I couldn't help notice the humans everywhere."

Sin chuckled. "I wasn't trying to hide them from you."

"I thought letting humans know what we are was against the law."

"It is."

"My dad will have kittens when he finds out." I had no doubt he'd discover Sin's secret. Dad didn't rule

Lake City because he had a good heart. He was very resourceful and intelligent. I swallowed the lump growing in my throat. "Forget it. I don't care if he knows."

Sin tossed me an amused glance. "He knows."

"But—"

He pressed his fingers over my mouth. "These humans will never leave my nest. They volunteer to feed us for a chance to become vampire." He pointed to another human male whose mouth opened in a silent scream as he came. Small baby fangs protruded from his gums. "It takes five years if they can survive that long."

"Survive?"

"Accidents happen." He shrugged. "Samuel has been with us for four years. He's the oldest of my fledglings. He's more vampire than human. I think his flesh even burns under the sun now. Feed from him."

"He just came."

Sin raised an eyebrow. "You're not up to the challenge?"

"You didn't just say that."

He gave me a serious look. "I thought your body pumped fuck-me pheromones when you were hungry. I'm definitely not being affected by anything at the moment. Not like at the motel."

"I'd been starving for seven days when you found me. The room was full of the pheromones. I probably could have gotten a boner from a eunuch."

49

"Now?"

I shrugged. "This is the way I am on my regular day three. That's the day I should always feed on."

"Why?"

"Because I'm still in control and pick my lovers instead of the demon riding my ass like in the motel."

"So you're not strong enough to get a rise out of my fledgling? Good to know. I thought you were stronger than that." He stretched as if bored. "Let's get this over with. I want to sleep."

I got to my feet and undressed, tossing him a glare over my shoulder as I crossed the room toward Samuel the fledgling. I wasn't weak. I was picky. Like it or not, I had to feed. Better to take Sin's challenge, then go pout in my room until the demon took over again, and I found myself playing hide the salami with Rat.

Samuel lay resting on the pillows, his eyelids drooping in satisfaction. Vampires didn't age after they were made. He looked around the same age as us. His dark brown hair hung disheveled as if too many hands had run through it already. A sheen of sweat coated his pale skin that was dotted with bite marks in different levels of healing.

My heart pounded as I drew closer. Feeding from Sin and Cooper had rejuvenated my body. I could see that my ribs no longer striped my sides and the veins on the back of my hands were once more cushioned in flesh. I was starved, not ravenous. My demon didn't ride me like at the motel. I could walk away from this room.

By tomorrow, I'd be crawling back, though.

I had to accept what I was, which meant I had to feed from this young man, turning into a vampire. Kneeling next to him, I set my hand on his bare thigh. "Hi, I'm—"

He pulled me against him and rolled us until he was on top, pressing me into the cushions. His mouth trapped mine in an urgent kiss of soft lips and demanding tongue. He grabbed my wrists, pinning them above my head with one hand. The sharp tip of his baby fang caught on the corner of my mouth and the metallic taste of blood spilled onto my tongue. Samuel made an animal-like noise and licked at the small wound.

I could barely breathe or move.

Samuel spread my legs with his inhumanly strong hand. Sin was right. Samuel was more vampire than human. Did baby vamps know how to control their strength? Succubus power came from our beauty, not our muscles. I didn't want to be torn apart. He pressed his thighs between mine, his cock no longer limp. I wish I could say it was succubus powers and snub Sin, but it wasn't; my demonic nature lay partially satisfied. It wouldn't stir for another day. Samuel was just a horny boy.

I wished I could feed by just lying there and letting him have his way. Much like Sin had the first time he'd taken me. Achieving an orgasm when emotionally I was a train wreck would prove to be the biggest challenge of the day.

I couldn't do this. With a twist of my hips, I

51

struggled to push Samuel off. The baby vamp ignored me and tried to push his cock inside my pussy but he had poor aim.

Large strong hands encompassed ours and pulled Samuel's off mine.

I opened my eyes to thank Sin and met a stranger's gaze. Well, sort of a stranger. He was the guard at the entrance who hadn't liked seeing the chaffing around my wrists from the manacles.

He caressed the raw skin with a frown. "Easy, boy. You're not supposed to break the master's toy." The guard wasn't handsome. It looked as if someone had used his face to break cinder blocks but his rough hands held my arms so gently they barely touched. He still wore his jeans but his shirt, shoes and socks lay in a pile by the door next to mine. His delicious muscles held a sharp edge that came from hard work, not gyms.

"Finished with work?" It sounded obvious as soon as it came out of my mouth but his smile was worth it.

"Sun's up and I don't tan well. The wolves cover the day shift." He lay next to me and ran his hands over my arms.

Samuel shook his head. "Mine."

"There's enough for both of us." The guard set Samuel's hand on my breast. "Gentle. Don't mind him. At this age we're all cock and fangs."

The almost-vampire molded my breasts in his hands, pushing them together to lick and suck without moving his head much.

I gasped and rested my head on the guard's chest. "Do you have a name?"

He watched Samuel's play intently and I could tell he enjoyed it by the bulge pressing against my thigh. "Joshua."

I was doing it again. I was picking the nice one over the jerk. How could I stop the madness? Samuel wouldn't be able to feed me. He hadn't been turning me on until Joshua with the kind hands came along. I shouldn't have ever asked his name. That was mistake number one. I'd learn. First, I had to feed. Raising my head, I met Sin's stare from across the room. I mouthed *Can I have him too?*

He rolled his eyes and nodded.

I gave him a fake smile. It felt so unnatural on my face. The grin probably looked more like a grimace. I ran my fingers through the younger man's hair and gave it a sharp tug, pulling his attention off my breasts. "We're switching places." I'd had sex three times already today. If I was going to reach orgasm, we'd have to do things my way now.

Samuel nodded as I rolled to face Josh. The human pressed along my back, sandwiching me against Josh's broad chest.

I ran my hands over the bigger vampire's close-cropped military haircut and brushed my lips along Josh's. Tingles ran over the sensitive flesh and my hunger

53

uncurled in my lower abdomen. Oh yeah, this was better. The moans around us grew louder again. They caressed my libido, igniting my appetite. I let go of my angst before it tainted the energy that sex created for my kind, making it a bitter pill to swallow instead of a sweet feast.

I was a succubus. *I fuck, therefore I am.*

Samuel ran his hands over my hips. They traveled in between me and Josh when I sensed him undoing the other man's pants. I liked men who knew exactly what they wanted and Josh didn't seem to mind. This would be more fun than I'd hoped.

Both males ground their hips against me. I let one of my hands trail down to join Samuel stroking Josh's cock. Two hands were always better than one.

Josh crushed me to his chest and claimed my mouth, pressing our lips together and thrusting his tongue inside as if it were a promise of what he would do to my body later. He seemed to agree with my two-handed theory.

I squirmed and wiggled my way between them as I crawled my way lower. I left a trail of kisses in my wake. Every time I glanced up, Josh's stare had never left me.

Samuel seemed to understand what I was wanting instinctively. He set me between Josh's legs so I faced his cock.

I took a quick lick, listening to his hiss of pleasure.

The almost-vampire guided me onto my knees, stuffing pillows under my hips to raise my ass in the air so he could grip me properly. The hunger had me in its firm grip so I purred and tipped my hips. I was very ready for him.

Taking Josh's cock in hand, I circled the head with the tip of my tongue. I wanted to see the much larger, stronger vampire unravel and surrender to little old me.

My sisters made men beg. Their lovers gifted them with cars and jewelry. They took what they wanted from their men and dropped them like trash once they were done. I was tired of being weak and helpless. I needed that power. I needed to be heartless.

Slowly, I slid his tip just past my lips.

Samuel, on the other hand, was not so gentle with me. His fingers dug in my hips as he positioned his cock at my entrance. He panted with eagerness and thrust inside me with a blissful burn.

I groaned around a mouthful of Josh and raised my hips even higher to squeeze Samuel with my secret muscles.

The young man made the most exquisite noises. It must have been him I'd heard earlier when I'd been in my room, so full of desperate passion and need. He pumped his hips with urgency.

I swallowed Joshua's cock as far as I could and matched Samuel's rhythm. Sliding Josh in and out, fast and hard, desperate to taste him.

Josh tangled his fingers in my hair, his back arching as he thrust his hips, fucking my mouth. His lips moved in silent ecstasy.

I let them take over and floated in my own bubble of salacious delight. It had been a while since I'd worked two men into a frenzy and the empowerment was heady.

Joshua came, my name falling from his lips over and over as his seed hit the back of my throat. I clenched my mouth around him, sucking him deeper, making it last.

I was on the precipice of joining him, the sweet, heavy feeling of climax on the edge of crashing over me.

Samuel thrust so hard, his cries crested and it sent me over the edge into my own orgasm. I bucked against him, meeting his demanding need until he collapsed on my back.

As I lay sandwiched, my head resting on Josh's stomach, their flavors mingled inside of me and I couldn't separate them. I tasted violence and blood and bubble gum. I blinked. It was an odd combination.

Samuel rested his head on my back. "Keep?" He hugged me tight.

"No keeping. She's mine." Sin knelt next to us and untangled me from the men. He scooped me into his arms. "Full yet?"

I nodded. Even if I wasn't, I didn't think my body could take much more sex. "I don't think I've ever fed three times in one day."

"So you can feed from both of them at the same time?"

"Sure. Why would I have bothered if I couldn't?"

"For pleasure?"

I laughed quietly. He didn't understand. Sex for my kind was never about fun. It was about survival. I would have thought a vampire would understand. "When I orgasm my body creates energy and it uses the sexual energy of my partners. No matter how many, but it still counts as just one feeding." I frowned. "There's no cheating when it comes to demon nature."

Sin carried me into my room and tucked me into bed. "Stay in your room until nightfall or I come and get you. I haven't had a chance to introduce you to the shifters guarding the upper floors. I'd hate for them to mistake you for a snack."

"Thanks, Sin."

He sighed. "Zur-Sin." Brushing my hair from my face, he kissed my cheek. "Will you need to feed tomorrow?"

"No, not for three days. Now that I'm topped off I'll only have to feed every three days."

Chapter Six

Day Three of my cycle

Smoke billowed out of the toaster oven and set off the fire alarm. The piercing noise stung my eardrums as I turned on the water full blast and aimed the sink sprayer at the small flames consuming my pizza.

A stranger rushed to my rescue, waving his arms, and knocked the sprayer from my hand. He then unplugged the toaster oven, pulled out my burned breakfast, and blew out the flames. "Are you trying to kill yourself?" His glasses were out of whack and tilting to the left. Big green, angry eyes stared at me through them.

I reached out and straightened his glasses. The least I could do for my hero.

"You never spray water on an electrical appliance when it's plugged in. You're lucky you didn't get electrocuted." He held out the blackened disk and grimaced. "Are you the one setting off the fire alarm in here the last few weeks?"

I crossed my arms. "I did a few times. I can't be responsible for all of them." Come on, I couldn't be the only one setting fires in the nest.

Gigi stuck her head in the kitchen and rolled her eyes. "Again? You're a fire hazard, Pia." She eyed the man and gave him a shy smile. "Hi, John."

"Hey." He absently tossed my breakfast in the trash.

I watched my meal vanish. It was my day to feed and Sin had been busy with meetings all evening so he hadn't assigned me anyone to feast on yet. Food helped stave off the sexual hunger pains. Bye bye breakfast.

Gigi left before either of us could say another word. I sighed. She was so submissive that it was bringing out *my* inner alpha male, but Sin said I couldn't touch her. No matter how much I had begged. "Thanks for saving me." I'd been living in the nest for three months now. Every three days Sin would tell me who I could feed from. I didn't like feeding from someone I'd already used. I found it hard to meet their gazes as I'd pass them in the hall. They learned quickly that no matter how many gifts or poems or attention they lavished upon me, it was Sin who controlled my feeding habits. It helped ease some of my guilt. Some of it…

Suddenly, I lost my appetite. It must be the thick smoke in the kitchen.

"Breakfast at 11:30 PM? I guess you're vampire bait." He sounded less than impressed.

"No, but since I live under their roof I follow their rules." Most of the time. I had gone to the upper levels one afternoon to look at the wolf shifters and almost got my nose bitten off. Sin hadn't said anything to me

59

about it yet. I slept during the day and was up all night. It was an amazing way to avoid my family.

He leaned against the counter. "I'm John."

I grinned. "I gathered that when Gigi called you by name."

He blushed to the tips of his ears. "I work for Zur-Sin. I'm his IT guy. The computers said there were an unusual amount of fire alarms the last three weeks."

"Only the last three?" What a coincidence. I'd been bored enough to try cooking as a hobby these last few weeks. John had the whole geeky package going for him, right down to the pocket protector. "So are *you* vampire bait?" I didn't see any bites but I knew from experience that necks weren't the preferred source for feeding.

He shook his head. "Vampires don't like to feed off my kind."

Sin stormed into the kitchen. "Stop setting fires!"

"Sorry."

"You're banned from the kitchen. Someone will make your meals from now on." He hit his chest with both hands. "We tend to be flammable." His gaze traveled to John. "You're not feeding from the demon. Get dressed. I'm taking you to Cleaver tonight." He left without giving me a time frame, which meant he wanted to leave now.

I blinked at the skinny, messy-haired man in front of me, who examined his worn running shoes as if they were the most interesting thing in the kitchen. Demons didn't like my kind. Most would have killed me on sight. I gulped and took a step back.

"I heard he was keeping a succubus in the nest. I thought it was just rumor." When he glanced up at me I didn't see anything but pure curiosity. "My mother told me to stay away from girls like you."

A hysterical laugh escaped my mouth and I clapped my hands over it. Mocking demons was suicidal. I hurried toward the doorway, knocking my glass of milk off the counter with my elbow. The plastic cup bounced on the floor and the milk exploded everywhere. "Shit." I grabbed a roll of paper towels and bent to clean it at the same time as John grabbed a dishtowel.

We knocked heads on the way down and I landed on my ass in the milk. I rubbed the bump forming on my head. "Ouch."

He knelt in front of me. "Are you all right?" Touching my sore head, he made it hurt more.

"Ow, ow." I laughed again. "Are you the demon of kitchen mishaps?"

He gave me a shy smile that curled my toes. His glasses were crooked again. If he were anything but a demon, I'd stuff him in my pocket and take him out to pet as needed.

"I thought fire and brimstone was the *in* thing for demons."

He glanced down at his torn jeans and short sleeved button-down shirt. "I'm not much of a fashionista." John didn't inspire fear like Sin did. If anything, he seemed harmless.

I listened for anyone outside the kitchen. At this time of the night most of the nest was empty. The vampires went out to hunt or work for Sin, and the humans had chores to do before the vamps came home. I'd been a good succubus for Sin, feeding when told and with whom he chose. I had kept a smile pasted on my face for months even though my insides rung with emptiness and I talked about nonsense, not wanting to dwell on anything that might spark my memories. On the outside, I seemed like the old me. On the inside, I was shattered and vulnerable. It was late on my day three, I was hungry, and John's rescue chimed all my buttons. Sweet, shy, and cute. A deadly combination.

Sin had me feeding off gorgeous vampires and shifters so full of their own beauty that they tasted like *Twinkies*. Artificial and unhealthy. I needed meat and potatoes. John interested me. He had made me *laugh*. I couldn't remember laughing for real since I'd arrived here.

Without a second thought, I leaned forward and gave him a chaste kiss.

His eyes went wide. "Zur-Sin said no." Oh my god, if he got any cuter I was going to drag him to my room and have all I could eat night. I would have thought the cold milk soaking my panties would have cooled me off.

"Do you do everything Sin tells you?" I got to my knees and slid in the liquid as I pushed John to sit on the floor against the counter. I straddled him and pulled off my shirt.

"Y—yes." His gaze stayed riveted on my bra and he licked his lips. "He's going to kill me."

"For feeding me?" I undid his jeans. "He's late in providing me any candidates and I don't think I can wait any longer." I really didn't. Hunger coursed through my veins, setting my teeth on edge. Maybe John's mother was right. He should definitely avoid girls like me. I slid my hand inside his jeans and wasn't disappointed by what I found.

He closed his eyes. "Pia, there are cameras in this room."

I hesitated. The hunger beat at the walls of my conscience. I was a succubus. What kind of succubus could afford a conscience? A dead one. I had to feed. Now. All these weeks Sin and I had kept things under control. He'd gotten lax tonight. That's how fast the demon part of me snapped.

"Not that I mind." He breathed heavy. "I just wanted to make sure you knew we'd be recorded." His thoughtfulness tipped the balance. I couldn't control it anymore.

I lunged and tore his shirt open, buttons pinging off kitchen appliances.

He in turn snapped my bra open and fondled the girls with shaky, eager hands. "I am going to pay for this later."

After weeks of feeding on a regular schedule, I had filled out back to my normal size. My sisters were stop-traffic-on-a-bad-day kind of beautiful, but I wasn't a slouch.

With a practiced ease, I shimmied out of my pants and underwear while John pawed and kissed whatever he could reach. A girl could get used to this kind of worship, even from a demon.

He pulled me back to the floor and crawled on top of me. "Are you wearing glamor?"

"No, we don't have that kind of magic."

"You're so beautiful." He kissed me, exploring my lips with keen, excited enthusiasm. He moaned and slid the tip of his cock to my entrance, teasing me by slightly pressing in and out.

I was so wet and ready for him. He didn't need to be this gentle. My mothers always warned me away from demons, saying they'd rape and kill me for just being a succubus. I was beginning to believe them, because John was killing me softly.

He pushed farther inside with a groan and licked along my bottom lip, sending tingles straight to my aching pussy.

I raised my hips and gripped his ass, sliding him deeper.

Sensing my urgency, John rose on his arms and fucked me like a demon on a mission. He plunged so deep and hard I couldn't breathe to make a sound. I clung to him and held on for the ride. Small inhuman snarls escaped his lips.

Like a ninja warrior my orgasm snuck up and

jumped me unexpectedly. It hit with such force, I arched back with a scream. The white light of bliss blinded me as I became a slave to my sensations, bucking and clawing under his weight. He tasted of wind and heat that warmed me from the inside out as we created magical energy.

John roared and reared up, almost bending in half as his hot seed splashed against my womb. "Oh yes." He breathed and fell on top of me. He pulled out and rolled off. "Oh yes."

I glanced at the clock on the stove through the haze of left-over smoke. "Crap, I better hurry. Sin hates waiting for me." I jumped to my feet and wiped the milk off my limbs with my shirt. "Thanks, John. I needed that."

"Anytime." He waved weakly and closed his eyes.

I didn't bother to dress as I hurried to my room to change. Most of the nest had seen me naked anyway.

Chapter Seven

"I don't know why you're so mad at me." I sat in Sin's car as he zoomed through the dark streets of Lake City toward Cleaver, a private BDSM club that catered to only the paranormal community. I didn't frequent the bar. I made a terrible submissive and my dom skills were lacking. "I was hungry. You can't leave me waiting so long on my day threes. It's not like I have control."

"He's a *mazzikim* demon." The vampire squealed into the parking lot, almost crushing a couple crossing to the club.

"Oh." My heart skipped a beat. "He doesn't look like one."

Sin parked his car and rested his forehead on the steering wheel. "Glamor, Pia. He's wearing glamor."

"I fucked a mazzikim demon?" And lived. The mazzikim were the pillage and violence kind of demon. They fed off pain and despair. My stomach rolled. John didn't give off that kind of vibe. He hadn't even hurt me except when he'd purposely poked the bump on my head. Yeah… "If he's so dangerous, why is he in the nest and working for you?"

"Because I'm more dangerous than he is. John won't cross me and live."

I clutched his arm. "You're not going to kill him

because of me?" What had I been thinking, seducing John? Sin acted as if he owned me and in many ways he did. I'd crossed a line and now John would pay for it. The demon's mind had probably been filled with my fuck-me pheromones when I'd propositioned him. His kind hated mine and this was probably why.

Sin stared out the windshield, his jaw solid as granite.

"Please." I bowed and rested my forehead on his lap. "It's my fault. Don't do this. I have enough guilt."

"You're supposed to feed only on those I assign you."

"I'll do better. I promise." It wasn't all my fault. He'd waited too long to feed me.

Sin pulled out his cell phone. "Is he already dead?" He paused. "Let him go, and I want him back to work tomorrow." He cut the call and lifted me from his lap.

I wiped a tear from the corner of my eye before he saw it. Crying made him even crankier. Sin had never raised a hand to me but he knew how to hurt me in other ways. This was as much my punishment as John's. How would I ever make it up to the demon? I cleared my throat. "What does John do for you?" I did my best to sound nonchalant and failed.

"He's good with computers and needs a place to hide. As long as he makes me money, he can live in Lake City."

"How does he make you money?"

Sin glared at me. "By doing what he's told." He got out of the car and stalked to my side to open the door. Normally, I wouldn't have waited but with Sin in such a bad mood I didn't dare jump out like normal. He was an old-fashioned vampire with an odd sense of honor. He liked taking care of me, I could sense that, but if I pissed him off enough he'd pull out his box of *bad* toys.

He offered me his hand and helped me out of the car. His gaze traveled over the red leather outfit I'd found on my bed. With a little lube, I was able to squeeze into the pants and matching top that wasn't much more than cups in the front with laces holding the girls in place. I'd be fine as long as I didn't jump up and down or sneeze. "You look good." He ran his fingertips along my exposed flank before snaking his arm around my waist possessively.

"Thanks. So do you." Sin always looked great. He could be dripping in blood and still make it look stylish. Tonight, he wore black leather pants and vest that strained against his chest. "I didn't mean to make trouble, Sin."

"Zur-Sin." He spoke with an edge of growl to his voice. "Trouble seems to be your middle name."

I stared at my red heels as we walked to Cleaver's front door. He was right, but for the wrong reasons. I'd proven I had terrible judgment when it came to men, and poorer control when it came to my demon nature. It was so hard to resist males who were nice to me.

The bouncer let us in without a cover charge. People respected Sin, or feared him. We never waited in line or couldn't find a table. He'd been meeting with many of the community leaders since obtaining his new title of co-ruler and had broken ground on new club for his nest called Suck. He was a busy vampire.

The smell of sex filled the inside of the club. Thank goodness I'd already fed. Tables and chairs surrounded the bar where we entered with a few couches to the left that most doms used for after-care and snuggling. A small empty dance floor was to the right, but who came to Cleaver to dance? The dungeons were to the back of the club behind the bar where Samantha, the dungeon mistress and owner, monitored the scenes being played by her customers. Samantha was part of my father's charm and didn't like me much. Not many succubi did. Not since I'd forced my father to lose half his power to Sin.

The vampire paraded me to the bar and settled me on a stool. "Since you've already fed, what do you want to do?"

I wanted to curl up in bed with a tub of ice cream and watch bad reality television. "I could flog you?"

His frown implied he still hadn't forgiven me and wasn't in any mood for my jokes.

"You could flog *me*?"

He shook his head. "I don't play well with others, not unless they can take damage." He wasn't even looking at me. He had his eyes on a dom across the room who wore one of those scary leather masks. "My date is already here. You should be able to find someone eager to play your games."

69

I sighed. "Anyone specific?" It wasn't above Sin to ask me to seduce a business prospect or competitor, and I wasn't making the same mistake twice in one night by picking my own playmate.

"No."

"Then why bring me here?"

"It's your day three. I thought to kill two birds with one stone, not for you to jump a demon in my kitchen." He shook his head again as if he *still* couldn't believe what I'd done. "Take the night off. Go play." He frowned. "Don't burn the place down." He left me alone at the bar and strode across the room to the dom, running his hand over the man's shoulders as he whispered in his ear. Sin liked both men and women. He didn't like sharing, though. He would rather watch me with another before joining to make a threesome. I wouldn't be welcomed on his date.

I ordered vodka straight up and sipped. I should have stayed home. Odd that I considered Sin's nest home now, but I could barely even think of my family without tsunami-sized waves of guilt. I tossed the remainder of my drink back and let it burn all the way to my stomach. I didn't need a family, I had a nest. Waving to the bartender, I held out my empty glass for a refill.

Families were for humans. My parents had made a huge mistake by sending me to mortal school. They thought my sisters and I could learn to mingle better with our prey by growing up among them. It worked great for them. My sisters hunted their territories with grace and tact. Hell, they hunted my territory as well, since I wasn't using it. I drank my second vodka without tasting it.

Twisting in my seat, I faced the BDSM crowd. No one would bring humans here. Against house rules and dangerous for the mortals. Samantha enforced the use of safe words, but the paranormal community considered certain extremes a norm. Most of them could take major damage and heal within hours.

Sin led his dom toward the dungeons. He kept a private room there. Vampires considered blood foreplay. I'd tried to watch once but didn't have the stomach for it. Sin was a sadist and I was a wimp. He also liked his playmates dominant and the thing that puzzled me was he never lacked for volunteers.

A young selkie sauntered passed the bar from the dungeons. He had an after-orgasm glow. I recognized him because he was my sister Adele's favorite snack and sub.

My heart leaped in my throat. She didn't share her subs and none of them would dare cheat on her. I slid off the bar stool and scooted to the other side of the bar before he spotted me. If he was here, my sister would be too. Lucky for me he seemed too dazed to notice me scoot to the dungeon as he flopped onto an empty couch. I hovered at the other end of the bar until I spotted Adele striding from the scene room, cleaning her hands with a wet wipe.

Her long dark hair hung to her waist in smooth waves I could only dream about. She wore a dark leather dress that ended below her knees. She hesitated by Sin's room and pounded on the door.

71

Sin cracked it open. "What?"

"Do you have my sister in there?"

"No."

She bit her bottom lip as she tried to peek past him.

"I'm not lying, Adele. I promised your family I wouldn't hurt her."

"You're not known for keeping your promises."

"No, but I'll keep this one. Your sister is too broken for me to have fun with. I left her at the bar. You can ask her yourself." He slammed the door shut in her face.

Adele hurried on her stilettos to where I'd been. Seeing her was the last thing I needed on this fucked-up night. The nail in the coffin, per se. Why did she care? Being the middle child, Adele always had a chip on her shoulder. Picking on me had always made her feel better, but god forbid anyone else tried. She was an assertive, gorgeous, big-hearted succubus.

Where I was nothing.

I strolled in the opposite direction, going deeper in the dungeon. Lots of customers came out on Saturday nights, so I had plenty to watch. Most stations were in use. I wish I could feed off other people's climaxes because this place could be a drive thru for my kind. I wandered from station to station, not really watching anything in particular. No, I had the pleasure of using people like John, in front of a camera no less. How did he feel about that? At the time, I knew he didn't care but afterwards when clarity returned, regret would set in. I knew regret had rooted its way into my conscience.

What kind of person had sex with strangers in a kitchen? The kind who lay in wait for the married postman to show up then seduced him right in her own home. Sharp pain stabbed my chest and I couldn't move. I slumped onto one of the benches lining the wall. I'd promised myself to forget the past but no matter what I did it snuck up on me. I thought if I stopped remembering and stopped feeling it would all go away, but the emptiness I sought wouldn't remain.

I glanced over my shoulder in the direction of Sin's closed door. I should tell him to take me home. This place, my sister, and John were shredding me apart. If I interrupted Sin, he'd get even angrier though.

He told Adele the truth when he said he wouldn't hurt me. Part of me wished he would, and deep down inside that's why I had really agreed to live in his nest. That maybe he or one of his other vampires would finish what I had started in the motel, but he'd told Adele he promised not to hurt me. In other words he'd sworn to protect me, even from myself.

Maybe it was time for me to leave the nest and strike out on my own again. Nothing linked me to Lake City anymore except my family, who I didn't ever want to see again. I could borrow some money from Sin and head south. I heard there was another charm of my people in Howdin, close to the beach. I could rock a bikini.

I'd have to figure out the whole feeding thing

again. There wouldn't be anyone to tell me who to use. Those decisions would be all mine. Again. Until I fucked up when the first nice guy gave me flowers or called me smart. Could I resist falling in love again? I didn't think so and I'd probably make all the same mistakes.

Rising back onto my feet, I went further into the dungeon and away from the temptation of Sin's private room. This part catered to the more hardcore patrons. Even Adele didn't play in here. The distant snap of a whip followed by grunts was the only noise. Not even the music from the bar drifted this far.

I stepped close to the St. Andrew's cross screwed to the wall with thick steel bolts. It was constructed of old, nicked wood like untarred railroad ties and gave off a vibe of age. Not abnormal in a place run by old creatures. I ran my fingertips over the rough surface. Out of the corner of my eye I spotted someone watching me a few feet away. I tried not to jump. Damn vampires could be near silent when they wanted. I twisted to face him. "Can I help you?"

He gave me a crooked smile. "That's my line."

Chapter Eight

"Am I breaking a rule?" I glanced at Cleaver's walls around the cross for a *do not touch* sign.

"No, but you seem…" He shrugged. "Sad." Cropped close to his head, his dark hair gave him a menacing appearance. He wore jeans and a red t-shirt because he didn't need the leather costume to show his dominance. It oozed off him.

I cleared my throat and pasted on my best fake smile. "Nope, I'm fine."

"That's a bald-faced lie." He approached me, blocking my escape off the small staging area. "People who lie deserve to be punished."

My mouth opened but nothing came out. He was right. I was a liar. I'd lied to Pierre and I lied to myself. I was pressed against the cross now as he leaned closer to me. "Do you belong to Zur-Sin?" I'd lived in the nest long enough to recognize the vamps who lived there.

"All vampires in Lake City belong to him but I'm old enough not to need to live in his nest. Do you belong to him?"

75

"No." It came out so quietly I doubted anyone without supernatural hearing would have heard it.

He took a deep breath as if savoring it. "That's almost truth. I won't poach the master's playmates."

"I'm his…" What the hell was I to Sin? Not his girlfriend, or even his friend. He took care of me, gave me shelter, and fed me. My stomach twisted in knots. "I'm his pet." That didn't really label me well either, because most people loved their pets. "He doesn't own me." There. That covered what I really wanted to say.

"You look like a bad girl." He set his hand on my bare midriff.

"Why would you say that?"

"Because only bad girls wander back here." Or stupid ones, his voice implied. "People have been known to get punished for less in this part of the dungeon."

I held my breath. He wanted to hurt me. I could see it in his eyes. He had the same look Sin got when he discussed his *hobby*. Icy fear coursed through my veins and sent chills along my spine. If I screamed for help, someone would hear me, but who would care? I blinked at the stranger hovering over me. That's what it all came down to, the story of my life. Those who did care about me shouldn't and those I wanted to care about me didn't. I'd never been so alone.

He pushed me toward the exit. "You should go back to the bar, little girl, and learn better manners."

"Maybe I want you to punish me." It was the least I deserved. I'd wrecked not just my life but Pierre's and the postman's. He'd been married when I'd torn the clothes off his back. I'd been so far gone with hunger, my pheromones took over the postman's mind and he'd taken me on the floor by the front door. Last I'd heard his wife had filed for divorce. "Like you said, I'm a bad, bad girl."

A spark of interest flashed in his gaze. He lifted his chin and assessed me. "Have you done this before?"

"Sur—" I stopped my lie. He'd know. "My sister is Adele Blyton. What do you think?"

He laughed, throwing his head back. "A succubus? Is this your day three?" His invitation just about caressed my skin.

"I already fed."

"Too bad." He spun me around. "Assume the position."

I set my hands against the cross and spread my feet. My heart ached with intense pounding. Maybe after this I could finally start forgiving myself, since ignoring my past was doing nothing for me.

He undid my leather pants and pulled them off, making sure to run his hands over my ass as he bent to slide my feet out of them. Thank goodness I'd worn a thong. I usually went commando but leather could chaff my important bits. He leaned against my legs and bit my left cheek.

"Hey!" I almost swatted him but caught my arm in the down swing and set it back against the cross. Fangs hurt; don't believe those stupid vampire movies.

He saw what I'd almost done though. "You're feisty." He rose behind me and undid the laces of my top until it fell at my feet, letting my breasts fall free. "I don't like that." Grabbing my hands, he restrained my wrists in the soft leather cuffs attached to the cross. He did the same to my ankles. "This should help you behave." Silence settled around us except for a distant weeping that had replaced the earlier cries.

I hung my head. How had I lost my way and gotten so far from who I was? Who had I become? I wasn't liking her much. My parents taught me about love. I'd seen it all my life. I was raised with it. How could I not want it for myself?

He returned just as silently as he had left but this time he carried a metal suitcase that he set upon a table. I guess Sin wasn't the only person who owned a box of bad toys. Sin's looked more worn though. My dom held a paddle. "We'll start slow. What's your safe word?"

"Stake." Of the wooden variety.

I sensed him go very still. "Smartasses get extra punishments. What's the house safe word?"

I rolled my eyes. "Red."

"And if you want me to pause?"

"Yellow."

"Good, let us begin." He swung the paddle and let it connect with my behind.

I gasped at the sudden sharp pain. He didn't hold back on his vampire strength. It stung right down to my bones.

He repeated his swings, not following any pattern or rhythm until I cringed with each breath. He paused and ran his hand over my hot, sensitive skin. "Are you still bad?"

I bit my bottom lip to stop from moaning from his touch. This was supposed to be punishment, not foreplay.

He slapped me sharply with his palm. "Answer me."

"Yes." I gasped out my answer.

"Good." He returned to his box and sorted through his equipment, testing them against the air. I followed every movement, trying not to picture how those tools would feel on me. He held up a soft flogger used to tantalize the flesh, and grimaced before approaching me with it.

"I want it to hurt."

He glared at me then at the flogger.

"I'm very bad. I need you to punish me."

A slow grin spread his lips. He tossed the flogger aside. "As you wish." Without hesitation, he pulled out a cane. I knew it because my sister owned one and had used it on me when I borrowed her favorite skirt without permission. They hurt.

I shrank against the cross and closed my eyes.

The first strike was the worst and I cried out. After that, I bit the inside of my cheeks, repeating *I deserve it* over and over in my head.

He worked the cane around my shoulders and stopped.

I panted. Sweat coated my skin. Gone was my original arousal, replaced by a deep ache. I expected pain, but in comparison to the emotional trauma I suffered, the bruises were almost a relief. I was replacing my inner discomfort with an outer one. "More," I whispered.

He brushed his fingertips over my cheeks and came away with my tears.

I clung to consciousness. The pain belonged to me. "I deserve this."

"What?" He stopped mid swing. "Did you use your safe word?"

"No." It came out a whisper and I licked my dry lips. "Hurt me."

He snarled. Returning to his position behind me, he worked the cane over me with renewed zest from shoulders to knees. The thwacking rhythm slowed.

"More."

He moved so he could see my face. "I don't know." He glanced over his shoulder as if looking for someone to ask. With gentle hands, he slid his fingers inside my thong. His eyes went wide. "We're done."

"No."

"Yes. You're supposed to be getting off on this. You're not." He unclasped my left wrist.

"Please, don't stop." I kept my wrist where it was. "I promise to do better."

"Pia?" Sin's voice struck me as sharply as the cane. A snarl followed and I sensed my dom's grasp on my restraints yanked away. "What are you doing to her?"

"S—she asked me to, master." The dom lay on the floor next to me. "She wouldn't use her safe word. I stopped it when I realized what she was doing."

"What *was* she doing?'"

"Making me punish her for real, not for pleasure. Please, master. I didn't know."

"Sin, it's okay. Let him finish."

He didn't listen to me and undid the restraints holding me to the cross.

I puddled to the floor before he could catch me.

"Fuck." Sin loomed over me. He held a blanket, I'd no idea where he'd gotten it from, and covered me. "What am I going to do with you, Pia?" He lifted me in his arms and I must have blacked out because the next thing I recalled was swaying in Sin's arms.

I closed my eyes against motion sickness. The ding of an elevator startled me and I sensed us moving again until I rested on something soft. I sank deeper into what must be my bed and listened as Sin spoke to someone.

"Flynn, we need to talk about Pia."

Chapter Nine

The metallic taste of blood woke me from a deep slumber. I blinked the sleep from my eyes and wiped my mouth. My hand came away wet with an unnaturally ruby-colored blood smeared across the back.

Sin sat on the edge of my bed. The wound on his wrist healed before my eyes.

"What did you do?" I sat up quickly and a wave of dizziness rolled my stomach.

With a finger set on my breastbone, Sin pushed me to lie down again. "Don't vomit in my bed." His frown grew impossibly stern. So I wasn't in my room.

The dim lighting didn't reveal much detail but I could see other rooms behind Sin through the doorway. "Where are we?"

"My apartment. We'll have more privacy."

I'd never been here before, but I knew his living space was off limits to almost everyone and that it was deep underground.

The room stopped spinning finally. "I'm good. What are you doing feeding me your blood?"

"Healing you." He rolled me onto my side and ran

his hand along my spine. "The bruises are already fading. What were you thinking letting a sadist like Tony play with you?"

The taste of Sin stuck to my tongue. "Do you have any water?" I'd been drowning in despair at the club and it still suffocated my heart. I'd seen my future. My kind lived a long time. Every three days I'd be with a new male with no connection and no love. I wished Sin had never found me in that motel. Centuries of being alone wasn't the life I wanted.

He handed me a bottle of water that I sipped.

I was only wearing my thong. "You carried me home naked?"

"You weren't in any shape to dress."

The caning marks on my thighs faded before my eyes and the pain went with it. "I didn't know vampire blood could heal."

"It only does if you're as old as I am. Most vampire blood would just make you sick to your stomach."

"It won't do anything else to me, will it?"

He cocked an eyebrow. "Everything comes with a price."

"So I'm your slave?"

"You've been my slave since you moved in my nest. No blood required for that. If you were human like those in my nest, you'd be compelled to do as I say." So that was how he kept the humans obedient.

"I wondered what was wrong with me that I couldn't seem to stay out of trouble like them. Maybe your blood will cure me."

"I doubt there's any cure for your troublesome nature." He kissed the top of my head.

I turned, giving him my back. "Leave me alone, Sin."

He sighed and rested his hand on my shoulder. He didn't correct my shortening of his name. "You've been living in my nest for months?"

I snorted. He didn't even know. "Yeah."

"Time passes differently for me, Pia." He sounded annoyed. "When you reach my age months are like hours, so forgive my disinterest."

I glanced at him over my shoulder. "How do you keep track of my day threes then?"

"I have a secretary. She sends me a daily agenda. Your feedings are scheduled by her."

"You're an ass."

He nodded. "That goes without saying. What I was trying to say is that you've been here for months and you haven't tried to contact your family once."

"How do you know? Are you tapping my cell phone?" I knocked his hand off me.

"Don't try changing the subject. I just spoke with your father."

I covered my face with my hands. "I don't *want* to

see them, okay?"

"I called him to ask permission to heal you." He spoke very softly. "I didn't know what the effects would be and didn't know how well you could heal naturally." For a succubus, I was pretty young. Power grew with age, just like a vampire, so I healed human slow and could die from trauma like them as well.

"Was it that bad?"

"You were just caned by a vampire who thought you were as old as Adele. Yes, it was bad." He massaged the bridge of his nose as if he had a headache. "Tony said you didn't use your safe word."

I wanted Sin's bed to swallow me whole. How did I explain? He wouldn't understand. He didn't even follow *time,* a basic law of physics. "I wasn't ready to use it." I tried to sound nonchalant.

"So he wasn't lying." He growled. His cell phone rang and he answered. "Let him go. He's not to return to Cleaver until I've discussed this with him further." Then he hung up.

I sat to face Sin slowly this time. "You're banning him because of me. It was my fault."

"It was both of your faults. You for not using your safe word, when clearly you had no intention to do so, and him for not realizing this." He stabbed me with his glare. "You're banned from there as well. No dom will trust you now."

"Not even you?"

He laughed. "Especially me. If someone doesn't tell me to stop, I won't. Why do you think I pick my playmates carefully?" He shook his head as if bewildered. "Why did you do it? I don't understand."

I stared at the dark red sheets. Sin's bed seemed so mundane compared to the vampire. I had expected it to be orgy huge with chains hanging from the ceiling and leather cuffs bolted to the headboard. This just looked like a place to rest with extra soft pillows. He had a stereo system and a television. I couldn't picture him doing ordinary things like watching the news or game shows. "How old are you exactly?"

"Old. Don't change the subject." He'd said something about Babylon and Google when we first met. I would check it out if they ever let me near the nest computers again. I mean, one little virus and my password was revoked. "If you won't speak to me, then at least speak with your family." He held up his phone. "Any of them." It almost sounded like a plea. He rested his head in his hands. "I'm not very good at this kind of thing."

"Talking?"

"*Caring*. Speak plainly and honestly. Tell me what's wrong or god help you Pia, I'll be forced to do drastic things like marry you off to the first incubus I meet."

I gasped. "You wouldn't dare." I couldn't imagine a worse fate. The last place I'd look for a husband would be among my kind. My parents somehow managed to find love, but lightning didn't strike twice in the same family. That's why I'd taken up with humans. They were really good at loving. Maybe, one day, I'd find a man who could love me for who and what I was.

"Pia." He voice snapped out the unspoken command.

I jumped. "Punishment!" It came out as a shout. I crossed my arms under my breasts. "Satisfied?"

Being male, his gaze followed my action.

I yanked the sheets at the foot of the bed to cover my body.

"Of course, I'm not satisfied. It's not in my nature." He grinned, not because he was happy but to shows his impressive fangs and to remind me of what he was. "I thought we'd taken care of your issues when I let you move in here."

"How?" I tilted my head. He'd forced me to leave the motel. "I would have been happier if you'd let me die."

He grew statue still. It was creepy.

I lay back in the bed again, curling into a ball with the sheets pulled to my chin. "I didn't ask to be saved. Y'all forced it on me and I'm *trying*."

He crawled under the sheets with me and wrapped his arms around me.

"This is all because of that guy, Pierre, the one you told me about?" I hadn't told Sin the mailman part of my story on our drive back to Lake City. It wouldn't help him to understand my issue any better than he did then and I didn't want to revisit memory lane.

"Yeah."

"What if I killed him? Would you feel better?"

"No." I snuggled deeper into his arms. He felt warm, so he must have fed at the club. "I still love him. It would make it worse." Who was he that I had to explain the obvious? "I miss him." I missed the way Pierre smelled after a shower or the feel of him in bed next to me, the way his laugh rolled from deep inside his belly and how easy it was to make him do it. We'd been very happy together. A twinge of sorrow struck my chest. "I miss being happy."

"It's a dangerous thing for a succubus to fall in love. I know your parents are unconventional but I would have thought they'd explained that."

"I didn't listen."

He snorted. "How comforting it is to hear that I'm not the only one you ignore."

"It's not fair, Sin. Why can they be in love and not me? Why can't I find what they have?"

"Because they've had centuries to perfect their marriage and they stayed within their own race. You're what? Twenty?"

"Nineteen."

He shuddered. "You make me feel ancient. I hate it. I can't even remember being human. How the fuck am *I* supposed to help you? My best advice is to kill the fucker and move on."

"I would agree but I'm the bad guy in this story. I'm the one who deserves to die."

"You can't fight your nature. You need to forgive yourself. You didn't ask to be what you are. You just have to deal with it."

"And then what?"

He shrugged. "You continue to feed on your day threes just like all of your kind."

"What if I fall in love again?" I rested my chin on his shoulder and wrapped my limbs around him. "It's easy, you know."

"Maybe for you, sweetheart." He sounded stunned. "From my experience, it's the hardest thing to ever do." With strong hands, he rubbed my back. "While you were unconscious, I had a long discussion with your father. Apparently, he understand you. I couldn't figure out why he'd decided to find suitors for you."

"They think I'm impaired?" *Nobody* used suitors anymore. "No, Sin, don't let him do that."

"After what you just told me, I have to agree with him. A chosen circle of men you can feed from. That way you won't expose yourself to anyone you might like too much."

I clung to Sin's hand. Feeding from suitors was an old-fashioned thing that dated back to when my dad was just a kid. Back then incubi were more possessive of their wives and would only let them feed from certain males they deemed safe. After a few decades they became aware of how weak their wives were growing, and in turn they were too. The practice was abolished. As the old saying

89

goes, you are what you eat. If incubi wanted to remain strong their wives had to be well fed with variety, so they had to learn to share.

In my case, suitors weren't about possession. It was to keep tabs on me, making sure I didn't go on a starvation diet again or fall in love. They were treating me like I had an eating disorder.

"Where am I supposed to find these men?" My words came out mumbled since my face was buried in Sin's neck.

"Your father will be looking for candidates. I had a few suggestions."

I jerked from his arms and shoved him away. "My dad is going shopping for my lovers?"

Sin winced and rubbed his ear that was close to my mouth. "He said you'd say that. He asked me to remind you that it could be worse since legally he has the right to demand witnesses to make sure you've completed the act. If you don't want him involved, then get over Pierre and start acting sane."

"I hate you."

"I count on it. Otherwise how else could I be eligible for your suitors list? Your father wants men you won't be tempted to fall in love with."

Chapter Ten

Day two of my cycle

Feeding from just three men didn't bother me as much as the stigma of needing suitors. Word would spread, because nobody gossiped like my people did, and I'd never be able to look another succubus in the eye again. Present day, only insane or ugly succubi needed their families to contract suitors.

I had wanted to die before, but not from embarrassment. I sat in the common room while a ping-pong tournament went on around me. Vampires were very competitive. Sometimes the ball went so fast all I could see was a white blur.

Pulling out a crumpled piece of paper from my pants pocket, I went over the list of names. They were my suggestions from my dad, people I didn't really like but could bed. Since I was feeding exclusively off these three males none of them could be human. It would kill them.

The list was short.

Of all the people I'd fed from, couldn't one of them be decent enough for me to be eager to share their bed? I crumpled the paper in my fist.

Sin strolled into the room, paddle in hand. His gaze traveled to me tucked into the corner of a love seat. He grinned and joined me. "Are you playing?"

"Are you nuts? I can barely see the ball."

He opened my fist and pulled out my list. "My name isn't on here."

I eyed him. "You really want to be one of my suitors? You haven't fed me since the motel."

"Absence makes the heart grow fonder."

"My heart isn't supposed to be part of this endeavor into ancient traditions." I snatched the list from his hand and ripped it in two. "I hate this."

He leaned his chin on his hand. "You're not going to make this easy, are you?"

"Why should I?" I said it louder than I wanted and those around us suddenly grew quiet. "You seem to forget that this is *my* life." I pushed my way out of the room.

Sin caught me just outside the elevator and pressed me against the wall. His face was no longer amused. "Be careful how you address me in public. I've been very lenient because you amuse me, but that can end at any second." He gave me a little shake to emphasize his meaning.

I struggled to lower my glare. "I'm sorry." Pissing off the ancient vampire wouldn't get me anything but pain.

"Why are you making a list? Your father said he'd

take care of it."

"Would you be okay with that?"

"I'm not a complicated succubus brat."

I gasped. "I am not complicated. I'm sensitive."

Finally, the angry edge to his scowl vanished into a smile. "Is there someone specific in the nest you'd like?"

"For me to feed, I have to orgasm. So if I feel uncomfortable or unhappy nothing is going happen. There's got to be some chemistry."

"That's how people fall in love."

I swung my head back and hit it against the wall. "I know. So you can understand my predicament."

"That is quite a quandary." He rubbed his chin; the amusement had returned to his eyes. "A male who you like but won't love, who you're attracted to." His gaze grew heated and he pressed his hard, delicious body against mine. "You do like me, don't you Pia?"

All my girly bits ignited with instant lust. "Damn it, you know I do."

He ran his fangs along my neck, sending chills down my spine.

"Is there a point to this besides torture?"

His shoulders shook as he chuckled. "When your father decides to get something done he doesn't waste time."

"He picked them already?" My voice was pitched

so high I'm sure I heard glass shatter.

"Just one. It was an easy choice."

"Really? Who?"

"I'm not telling you." His smile was feisty and pure evil. Playful Sin was as much a jerk as cranky Sin. "But I'll bring you to his place and you can—uh—meet him." He held out his hand.

I stared at it dumbfounded then placed my trust in him by taking his offer.

"Let's be off." He tossed his paddle to Gigi, who waved good-bye.

"Can we take your motorcycle?" I'd been trying to get him to take me for a ride ever since I discovered he owned a Harley.

"No. Pick a different vehicle."

"I don't care then. Something that won't break down."

He tossed me an annoyed look. All his cars were well cared for. He let the nest use certain ones but he owned them all. In the security room he picked out the keys he wanted and led me to his fast, little silver bullet. He hated it when I called it that so I kept my mouth shut. The city streets still held enough traffic in the early night, which forced Sin to slow to human speed. It didn't take long to get to our destination.

I sat forward as we drove through the forested neighborhood. I recognized this place from the first night I'd met Sin. "We're going to Cooper's?" Since I'd moved into the nest I hadn't seen the shifter. "This isn't a good idea." I liked him way too much.

"Just spend the evening with him." He pulled up to the cabin.

I got out of the car and followed Sin to the front door, dragging my feet. Part of me was crying out *I don't want to.*

Sin knocked on the door.

Not long after, it opened. Cooper stood in the threshold framed by firelight, wearing only a pair of track pants that hung low on his hips. "Zur-Sin?" He rubbed his eyes as if he'd been asleep. It wasn't that late, was it? Then again, I'd been living on a vampire's timetable for a while.

Sin grabbed my arm and thrust me at Cooper.

If he hadn't caught me, we both would have gone ass over teakettle. He blinked at me. "Pia?"

"Hey, Cooper." I gave him a shy wave and tossed Sin a glare. The vampire hadn't even called ahead. Could there be a hole deep enough for me to crawl into? "Don't worry. I don't need to feed tonight." Oh my god, why was my mouth still running? "Not that I would mind." I squeezed my eyes shut.

The slam of a car door had me jerking them open again. Sin was pulling out of the driveway.

Cooper waved. "Bye, Zur-Sin." He gestured for me to come in. "Can I get you something to drink?" The entrance opened into a small eat-in kitchen, which

95

connected to a living room and fireplace. A few animal pelts decorated the log walls.

"Got anything with alcohol?" My hands trembled so I sat on them in the closest chair.

Cooper shook his head. "I don't keep any in the house. It lowers inhibitions and that doesn't mix well with the wolf." He tapped his chest. "I have water, milk, and hot cocoa."

I grinned. "Hot cocoa."

"Marshmallows?"

"Please." If Cooper was trying to seduce me, he was doing an excellent job by offering chocolate and sweets. "I'm sorry Sin dumped me on your front porch."

Cooper busied himself with cups and kettles. "Nothing surprises me anymore. He likes screwing around with me. He wants me to wolf-up and climb pack hierarchy." He chuckled.

"He used the words *wolf-up*?"

"Oh yes." The kettle whistled. "So how are you adjusting to vampire life?" Cooper fixed our drinks and sat across the table for me.

I shrugged. "Most of them ignore me unless it's my day to feed."

"Vampires are snobs. I've heard Sin doesn't let you feed from the shifters he hires."

"He fed me a few but…uh…you're all kind of possessive. It created problems." I got up and wandered around his living space. No television or desktop computer, lots of shelves stuffed full of books, no pictures of anyone special. It seemed empty and lonely.

Cooper joined me and sat in the only couch in the room in front of the fireplace. There was a pillow, a book, and a blanket next to him.

"Were you sleeping here when we barged in?"

He tapped the cushion next to him, inviting me to sit. "I fell asleep reading."

I picked up the book before joining him on the couch. I'd been known to turn a page or two. My eyebrows rose. "This isn't in English."

He plucked the book from my fingers. "I like to read great works in their original language."

"What story is it?"

"It's a philosophy book. I teach at Lake University." He watched me as if waiting for my reaction. A sexy philosophical werewolf who was a university professor. My succubus mojo just drooled.

"Do you wear a tie and a jacket with the leather patches on the elbows?"

He snorted his hot cocoa. "No."

"Too bad." I eyed him. "Would you wear them if I bought them for you?"

He threw back his head and laughed. "Are you offering to play the part of the scantily-clad student?"

I crawled onto my knees and leaned forward,

almost spilling my drink. "You know this game. I'm great at playing the bad girl. I can even pop my gum."

His smile faded. "You're serious."

"You're not?" I sat back on my heels. "Well, that was disappointing."

"Your father said you wouldn't need to feed until tomorrow." He took my half-finished cocoa and set it on the coaster next to his on the small side table.

"I don't." I twisted the hem of my t-shirt. If I'd known Sin was going to drop me off with Cooper I would have dressed up. Instead the shifter got slumpy Pia in flip flops and PJs instead. "So you met my dad?"

"Uh-huh. Woke up to him making breakfast in my kitchen. Almost set my house on fire."

My heart sank. "We have that in common." I kind of took after my father in that regard. "He's not forcing you to be my suitor, is he?"

"I had to interview for the position." Cooper winked.

"He knows you?" No offense to Cooper, but my dad didn't occupy his time by meeting low-level shifters.

"No. Zur-Sin apparently recommended me. Ever since that vampire discovered why I'm not interested in climbing ranks in my pack, he's been trying to help me in his own terrible and horrific way."

"Yes, I can understand this intimately, but does that have to do with my eating problems?"

"You're not my soul mate, Pia." He rested his

hand on my shoulder.

"Well, yeah, I could have told you that." I knocked his hand off. "The last thing I need in my life is for some shifter to think I'm his soul mate. Geez Cooper, don't try to stop my heart like that."

He tilted his head to the side as if confused. "Is that why you chained yourself to the bed before we found you?"

I glared at him until he grew still. I wasn't going to re-tell that story again. Going over those events with Sin had been hard enough, especially after how I felt at Cleaver. Forgetting my past was hard when everyone kept asking me about it. "You can say it's a symptom."

He cleared his throat. "So how exactly does this suitor thing work? Your dad didn't give me the details yet. He said a contract would be delivered tomorrow and I could read the details then."

"*Suitor* is a term my people use for a regular lover to feed from." There was a hell on Earth. "I'm having trouble." I took a shaky breath. "Emotionally." Tears burned in my eyes. "One—one night stands seem to be making things worse rather than better. My father thinks this will make me more stable." I had to trust Dad's judgment on this, since my original plan ended with me dead and Sin's idea of help just made me want to die. My family for some reason still cared about me no matter how hard I tried to shove them away. They understood what it was to be a sex demon. Maybe Sin was right, but I'd never tell him that, and I should pay my parents a short visit.

99

I missed them.

A tear spilled from my eye and I wiped it as fast as I could, hoping Cooper missed it. "I think you're a good choice." I shrugged one shoulder.

Cooper was so quiet that for a moment I thought he'd fallen asleep.

I peeked at him through my eyelashes.

When our gazes met, he gave me a small smile and pulled me into a hug.

"Are you still sorry you helped save me?" I mumbled against his solid chest. Being very muscular was one thing I could count on with shifters.

"Sometimes the roads we travel lead us to unexpected places. These surprises can either help or harm you. I think, Pia, you're here to help me too."

"Is this the shifter talking, or the philosopher?"

"We're one and the same." He chuckled and the sound rolled in my ear from his chest. "I think the reason I haven't met my soul mate is that I'm pretty shy around females. They make me nervous and those of my kind can smell it. Shifter females don't like the scent of weakness."

"You're not shy around me." I remember the way Cooper had taken me on the floor of the motel room. There wasn't a shy moment in that act.

"I know. Isn't that amazing?"

I smiled and snuggled closer to Cooper. "So you help me with feeding and I help you with girly wolves."

"Yes, just don't call them that to their faces. They might eat you."

"I think this a start of a beautiful friendship."

He handed me my cup of cocoa and clinked his cup against mine. "To friends with benefits."

"Cheers."

Chapter Eleven

Day three of my cycle

Once again it was my day to feed and Sin hadn't assigned me anyone, leaving me to fret. I locked myself in my bedroom, not wanting to jump someone like cute John again. I hadn't seen a whisper of the demon in the last three nights. Maybe he worked day shift like the werewolves?

I flipped through a fashion magazine I'd already read twice. The next time I saw Cooper I'd ask to borrow some books. Oh, maybe I should call him to feed me since Sin couldn't fit me in his schedule. Or maybe, I should call the vamp's secretary. She might have forgotten to tell Sin it was my day three. I reached for my phone as someone tried to barge through my locked door.

The frame shuddered. "Pia." Sin's annoyed voice traveled through the wood.

I raced to let him in. He hadn't forgotten after all. "Hey." I leaned against the door trying to act cool as my libido boiled in my gut. "Who can I feed from?"

"Hungry?"

"Starved."

He handed me a motorcycle helmet. "I thought I'd take you for a ride first."

I stared at it and blinked. "On your bike? But you said you didn't share."

He frowned. "Do you want me to change my mind?"

"No. Let me grab a jacket." The summer nights were warm but I imagined riding on the back of a roaring beast of metal I'd catch a chill. Sin was gone when I returned, so I ran through the nest and crashed through the security room out into the garage.

He sat on the Harley and patted the seat behind him.

I couldn't stop the skip in my step as I hurried to my spot and strapped my helmet on.

"Hold on tight." He revived the engine before taking off.

With my arms around Sin's waist and my head resting on his back, I watched the city speed by. The wind caressed my skin like a long lost lover and the bike vibrated between my legs. If it were alive, I would have asked it to be my next suitor. We drove out of the city and past the suburbs. The night droned past me in a haze of lights and shadows.

The road became a steep climb but the engine didn't even seem to strain. Oh, baby. Peeking around Sin, I saw the sign for Mount McGregor, the local national park. I hadn't been here in years. At the top was a make-out

103

point.

I ran my hands over his stomach, tracing his carved muscles through his t-shirt.

He tensed under my touch and accelerated faster toward the top.

I pressed my face to his back and smiled. He got my message.

We drove into Make-out Point but continued past the vehicles parked in the shadows. I'd spent a few evenings here in high school. It was interesting that Sin brought me here.

He slowed and coasted us past the parking lot and onto a trail.

"I don't think we're supposed to drive on this."

"Who's going to stop me?" He wound past the trees until I couldn't see the cars anymore. So Make-Out Point wasn't really our destination. Inching to a stop, he parked us in a clearing.

My breath caught in my throat and I swung off the bike to walk to the edge of the cliff. Lake City spread before us like a spider web made of golden lights. "I've never seen this view."

"Most people hike here during the day but it's best viewed at night." He hadn't followed me. "It's even better at Christmas when the tree is floating in the lake all lit up."

I held out my arms and took a deep breath. Who knew Sin had a romantic side?

"Take off your clothes, Pia."

Or not. I grinned and undid my jeans. It was my day three after all, and Sin did want to be one of my suitors. "Are you letting me take you for a test drive?" I took off my clothes and set them on the grass before turning to face him. He hadn't touched me since the night at the motel.

His gaze traced the lines of my curves and he made an appreciative sound. "I've been with many women but there's something irresistible about you." He clicked his tongue against his teeth.

"It's called pheromones." I slipped out of my panties and unclipped my bra, letting the moonlight bathe my skin. Strolling toward him, I did my best to ignore the sharp pine needles under my feet. My hunger for his body made it easy.

He met me halfway and stalked around me, taking me in from every angle. "Perfect."

I squirmed under his intense gaze. "Have you met my sisters?"

"Your sisters remind me of winter, where you, Pia, are like my sunshine." He pressed against my back and ran his hands over my arms. "You're filled with warmth and light that scald me." With light kisses, he followed the line of my neck to my shoulder. His hands moved to cup my breasts, kneading them together until he pinched my nipples.

I flung my head back against his shoulder with a gasp. Something about Sin was irresistible as well. Even on my non feeding days, he could lure me into bed. Would it be so bad if Sin was my suitor? So far he hadn't let me down once. I couldn't say that about most people in my life.

He moved until he stood in front of me, his finger trailing to my pussy and sliding into my entrance. "Always so ready for me." He purred and tilted my head back so he could claim my mouth.

Hard and deep, he stole away my breath, bending me back and thrusting his fingers in time with his tongue.

I clung to his shoulders and moaned. A shudder of pleasure ran through my body. I was so close.

He eased me into his arms as he straightened and withdrew from our kiss.

"What's wrong?" I searched the dark woods around us but couldn't see any lurkers.

"Go sit on my bike."

I did as he ordered, not sure how we'd progress to feeding me from this position, but I wasn't ready to complain. I liked the big bike between my legs. The leather seat still held heat and was soft with wear.

He got on behind me.

"You're not going to make me drive like this." I tossed him a curious glance over my shoulder. I wasn't shy about being naked. After having to undress in front of strangers every three days, the timidity got old.

"No, I'm going to ride you. Take hold of the handle bars." He unzipped his pants and moved around a little behind as if positioning. "Put your feet on the foot pegs and lean forward as if you were racing. Become one with the bike, Pia." He chuckled.

I did as told, a little nervous about balancing, but Sin had his feet planted on the ground.

He lifted my hips and aimed his cock at the edge of my entrance.

I hissed in anticipation and arched my ass into him. I needed him so badly. His early teasing just pissed off my demon nature. If Sin didn't feed me soon, I'd be forced to storm the parking lot for someone who would.

With a gentle push, he entered me slowly. He didn't thrust. He just kept pushing deeper and deeper.

I cried out at the burning ecstasy. "Oh god, oh god, oh god." I squeezed the handlebars, the muscles in my arms trembling.

Only when he was completely inside me did he draw back just as slow until he was all the way out. "Again?"

"Yes." It came out needy and breathless.

Repeating the act a few more times, he kept me on my toes, just on the edge of orgasm but never letting me reaching my goal.

"Sin, please." My skin was coated with the sweat of my desperation.

"I love it when you're like this." He set his hands next to mine on the handles, his cock still deep inside me. Then he began to thrust like he meant it. Sin was powerful

107

and used his strength, plunging with a demanding beat. He leaned against me, pressing me along the bike. "Oh yes." He groaned. With one hand, he reached between me and the seat, massaging my breast.

Sin knew how to touch a woman. I'd expected that with an old vampire, but his face always made me forget we weren't the same age. Hands of experience caressed and fondled all my girly places until I raised my hip and mewled like a cat in heat. I clung to the edge of completion and listened to Sin's hoarse breathing. He mumbled things in a language I couldn't understand that sounded so harsh. I did this to him. I brought him to the verge of losing control. I squeezed my inner muscles and let the sensation of Sin's cock take me over the cliff of my orgasm.

Energy swelled inside me. He tasted spicy and stung my succubus sense. The power in what he added to my energy sizzled and crackled. He didn't relent or hold back his strength like in our other encounters. He took me hard, his balls slapping against my pussy and fingers digging in my hips.

"Fuck, Pia." He cried out for anyone in the park to hear.

I rolled my hips over and over until he plunged his fangs into my neck.

He came inside me and drank at the same time as my orgasm struck. His moans were music to my ears. I'd never heard him make such pleasurable noises before. He let me go and withdrew from my body. With a gentle nudge, he guided me off his bike then back on the seat to spread my legs. He pulled out a handkerchief and wiped me clean.

"Thanks."

He kissed me. "No, thank you." He retrieved my clothes and helped me dress since my limbs still trembled from the force of my orgasm. It would be an interesting ride home. I hoped I didn't fall off the bike.

I settled behind him and he guided my arms around him. He kissed my fingertips before setting them on his chest. Resting my head against his back, I absorbed his strength. This seemed more than feeding. It felt like we were crossing lines.

It felt like love.

Chapter Twelve

Day one of my cycle

The sidewalks were filled with people this sunny afternoon. Cafes had their outdoor tables available for the shoppers bargain hunting through the boutiques, flower baskets hung on every street lamp, and the smell of cinnamon overwhelmed all other scents. This district was my favorite in Lake City. I took a risk being here. My mothers and sisters loved this part of the city as well.

I set my sunglasses back on my face and pulled the brim of my sunhat lower. After months of living in the dark, the sunlight hurt my eyes and stung my skin. My accessories had nothing to do with hiding or anything.

Sin had escorted me to my bedroom last night, after our ride to Mount McGregor, and had crawled into bed with me for a nap. I'd fallen into such a deep heavy sleep that when I woke in the late morning, alone, I couldn't return to my slumber.

I had the afternoon all by myself. Sin was asleep with the rest of the vampires, Gigi never left protection of the nest, I hadn't made friends with any of the humans, and Cooper worked. That left me and the credit card my dad had given me when I'd left for college. What to do, what to do?

Grinning, I set my four shopping bags by an outdoor table of the best pastry/coffee shop in the city. I'd spent a good portion of my time in a lingerie shop that was off the main strip and catered to those with more kink in their tastes. If Sin wasn't too busy tonight, maybe we could play fashion show. These kinds of things needed to be tested.

The waiter took my order and I leaned back into my seat and soaked in the noise of the city. I watched humans move around in their small herds. Some laughed, others whispered, and oh, one young couple were making out at the table across the street. I shifted my chair so I could observe without placing a crick in my neck. Young love was the best. No baggage, all full of wonder and experiment, totally unaware that they were making a scene. I grinned.

My coffee and cinnamon bun, smothered in icing, arrived. I picked at it with my fingers and savored the extra cinnamon this place added. After all the energy I burned on Sin's bike last night I deserved extra calories. I hoped to burn more tonight.

Sin treated me differently than the others of his nest. He wasn't exactly mean to anyone but he wasn't tolerant either. He gave orders, expected them to be done without question and he demanded results. Those who failed were punished. I'd seen the damage on their flesh. When I first came to the nest I'd expected to wear the same kind of wounds and walk with that pained waddle at some point, but Sin never disciplined me with pain. He

111

used withdrawal and pleasure instead. I could grow used to being his bad girl.

I swallowed my cinnamon bite whole and washed it down with my hot coffee before I choked. That last thought bordered dangerously on lines I shouldn't cross. Sin wanted to be one of my three suitors but if I allowed things to continue on this same path then my heart would be in trouble sooner rather than later. I couldn't afford another heartbreak. I was just mending the last one with Scotch tape. It would take more time and a lot more work before the tape became glue.

I continued eating without taste. Did I love Sin? I poked at my heart with an internal finger. Things seemed so muddled inside. I'd been so numb lately that any emotion, besides lust, seemed almost overwhelming. I'd have to tread lightly.

The couple across the street broke apart and I was about to raise my cup to them in gratitude when I recognized the man. My damaged heart pulsed, breaking away all the mending I'd done, and shattered into dust.

Pierre?

I set my cup on the table on its edge and it spilled across the blue tablecloth. The hot liquid dripped on my thighs but I couldn't move.

Pierre.

He'd found another woman already? I couldn't stop staring as he set his hand on her knee like he used to do with me. The oxygen around me seemed to have vanished and I couldn't draw in enough air. What should I do? I was torn between marching over there and kicking him where the sun didn't shine and crawling under my table until they left.

My chest constricted and the cinnamon bun rolled in my stomach. I was *not* going to vomit in public. I'd choke on it first. He attracted my gaze like the pull of a thousand suns and turning my head took epic inner strength that I hadn't known I possessed.

I clutched the table and caught my breath before I passed out. I thought he'd loved me as much as I'd loved him. Yet he obviously had moved on. Maybe I had loved him more? That didn't help. It only made the pain worse. I tossed some money on the table and grabbed my bags. The last thing I wanted was for him to see me. What was he doing in Lake City?

On weak knees, I hurried from the shopping district back to the car I had borrowed from Sin. I could make it. I could get home before falling to pieces. It was the weekend, so Pierre must have taken his new love on a romantic getaway here. I tossed my bags in the trunk then ripped the hat off my head and threw it inside as well.

"Pia?"

Dainty, well-manicured hands grabbed my shoulders and spun me. I'd inherited my birth mom's height so we could see eye to eye. She ran her hands over me as if checking if I were real. I'd never seen her so quiet.

A tear spilled along my cheek unchecked. I was so raw inside it wouldn't surprise me if I was bleeding to death. "Mom," I whispered. She was one of my three

113

moms but she was the one who'd actually carried me in her womb. They all treated me with the same amount of love but nothing was thicker than blood.

She hugged me so hard against her tiny frame I thought I would snap in half. "Oh my god, Pia." She kissed my head. "I've been sick with worry."

I sobbed, one loud awful sloppy noise, before I gained control again, even by the tips of my fingers.

She yanked away. "What's wrong?"

I pushed her away and stumbled against the trunk. My sunglasses fell off and she saw my tears. "Leave me alone." I scrambled to close the lid and hurried to the driver side door. The last thing I needed was her understanding. Didn't anyone get that? I didn't deserve it.

She dogged my steps, almost tripping both of us. "No, don't you dare leave me again." She slammed the car door closed and almost took off my fingers. She'd dropped her bags in her chase, her eyes wild and desperate. "What is that vampire doing to you?"

"Nothing. He's good to me." I stared at my feet. My tears trailed along my nose and dripped slowly one at a time.

She stroked my crazy curls, trying in vain to bring order to them. She'd done this for as long as I could remember. "Please come home. Please." Her voice shook.

Unable to speak, I opened the car door again and she let me. I climbed inside and drove away. Blinded by my tears, I'm not sure how I returned to the nest without crashing. I parked and made it through security.

None of the shifters said a thing to me as I hid behind my hat and bags doing my best to cover my distress. I bypassed my bedroom and took the second elevator to Sin's apartment. He'd given me the code.

I dropped my stuff on his leather couch, undressed as I walked and crawled into bed next to his cold, unconscious body. It spoke how much he trusted me that he'd give me access to him in his most vulnerable state.

Curled in a ball, I had an ugly cry on his shoulder. Pierre wasn't the only reason for my anguish. Seeing him only dented the dam I had used to bottle my pain; my mom sledge-hammered the rest away, and realizing I didn't love Sin crashed through the rubble like the Kool-Aid man. Oh yeah.

If it were Sin I'd seen at the café kissing another woman, I would have asked to join him, not fallen to pieces. I was in lust with Sin. I was in gratitude with him but not in love. Part of me wished I could be in love with the vampire. He wasn't possessive. He didn't mind sharing me. Open relationships existed, so why couldn't I make this one work?

I traced his beautiful face. It was only a mask. The man under it was someone I feared too much to trust with my heart. A creature as old as Sin couldn't possibly see me as more than just a toy.

Chapter Thirteen

Day two of my cycle

Most of the nest was out either hunting or having fun, which suited my needs. I wanted time alone. I loved my day ones and twos. It was the closest I came to feeling normal, almost human.

Seeing my mother yesterday had left me feeling hollower. Like someone had cut me open and used an ice scream scoop to scrape me empty. I hadn't spoken to any of my family members in months. Did I want to spend the rest of my life shunning them? It had accomplished nothing so far but hurt feelings. They deserved better, but once they found out what I had done they'd shun me instead. I guess in a sick way I had subconsciously decided to do it first.

My people took the sacred vows of marriage very seriously. Our whole culture depended on the symbiotic relationships between incubus husband and his succubus wives. If a wife had sex on a non-feeding day for non-feeding reasons it was considered cheating and punishable by divorce. She'd lose all her assets and his protection. The same went for a married incubus if he fed from a succubus he didn't plan on marrying. Seducing that married mailman was disgraceful. My being out of control wouldn't help my defense. *Another* of my many mistakes. Losing control of our demons could lead to humans discovering our existence, an even worse crime.

I hung my head and curled into a tight ball on the couch of the common room by the security area. People passed but no one used it or stopped. I'd discovered that if I wanted to be alone it was the best place to sit.

Once I explained my shame to my family, I'd be done with the guilt hanging around my neck. The ball would be in their court and they could decide if they really wanted to pursue my return home. Then my father could stop this ridiculous idea of suitors. I wasn't sure how to confess, though. Writing them a letter would be the easiest since I didn't have to respond to any accusations, but it was too impersonal. I sure as hell didn't want to call a family meeting. Maybe I should just confide in one of them first and go from there, but who?

Tossing my head back, I closed my eyes and tried my best to pretend I was on a beach far, far away. Sin wasn't any help. He thought I should just call my father and blurt it all out. Like he said, family wasn't his *thing*.

Someone entered the nest from the security room.

I cracked my eyelid open and spotted John.

Faded bruises shadowed his face and he walked with a slight limp.

I cringed. He must have taken quite a beating to still show signs of injury two days later. That, or demons

117

didn't heal as fast as vampires.

He stared at his phone as he walked and didn't even glance my way. C'est la vie of a succubus. *Fuck me and forget me.*

"John?"

He startled and caught his phone before it hit the floor. "I didn't see you sitting there." His eyes darted around the room. "Is Zur-Sin around?"

I shook my head. "No, he's deeper in the nest. I'm really sorry about..." I pointed at his face. "If I'd known..." Well, I had known. John had plainly said that Sin would kill him. I hung my head and stared at my lap. "I'm sorry. I was really hungry and you looked delicious."

Crushing silence filled the room. I glanced up.

John still stood on the other side of the room. "I knew Zur-Sin would want to kill me." He rubbed his chin and winced. "At the time, I didn't care."

"Those are my pheromones. I can't help that when I get hungry enough."

"I can see why my people avoid yours."

I nodded. How could I argue? He was right. My people were a danger to everyone. "You should have listened to your mother."

He snorted. "If I listened to my mother, I wouldn't be hiding from her."

"Families." I meant it as a joke but it came out more choked with emotion.

John hurried to my side and sat next to me.

The sudden dip in the cushions sent me falling against him.

He looked a little shocked at how I almost landed in his lap. "The cushions didn't look that soft." He tried to help me sit up but his hands ended up on my breasts and he yanked them away as if stung, then went for my shoulders only to manage elbowing me in the eye.

"Ow." I clutched my hand over the swelling orb.

"Oh, I'm sorry, Pia." He raised his hands up in defeat. "Really, I'm not doing it on purpose."

I pinned him with a glare from my one good eye. Mazzikim fed from pain and despair. I was an all you could eat buffet for John. "Sin told me what you are. You're very good at what you do."

"Hacking computers? Of course, I am. How else could I afford someone like Zur-Sin's protection?"

"I mean feeding from others."

"It was an accident. I swear." He set his hand over his heart as if that meant something to a demon, but it still made me laugh.

I rubbed my sore eye and straddled his lap. "Will it turn black like yours?"

He leaned forward. "I wouldn't know how to tell, but it's swelling. We should get some ice on it." With little effort, he picked me up in his arms and carried me down to the kitchen. I could have walked but I liked being carried by wiry and witty John. He set me on the counter and returned with an ice pack wrapped in a clean dishcloth.

"I thought you were supposed to put raw steak on a black eye."

"I don't think you want to smell like bloody meat with so many werewolf guards coming on later."

"Good point. I'll have to remember to ask Cooper if he would consider the smell an aphrodisiac like vamps do blood."

John's smile faded. "Who's Cooper?"

"My—my friend." I didn't want to say suitor. It held so many bad memories for my people and reflected my unhealthy state of mind.

"You're a terrible liar." He picked at a small hole developing on the knee of my jeans. "It's okay if you have a boyfriend. You just left so fast the other day that we never had a chance to discuss what happened between us."

My heart flip-flopped. "I thought you'd never want to speak to me again." Sin had almost killed John after I'd fed from him. Or was this some ploy for John to get revenge? The demon stood between me and the only exit out of the kitchen. Was this where John went full-blown mazzikim on me and stole me away to his hellish home? I hadn't realized what I'd been getting into when I jumped him to feed. "He's not my boyfriend in the way humans consider it. He's more like a friend with benefits."

"Lucky guy," he whispered.

"You think so?" I tugged at his long bangs. He

needed a haircut. "I mean, it can't go any further than being friends."

He glanced up at me. "Are you speaking about Cooper or us?"

"There can't be an us. Sin will kill you."

He shrugged. "That's up to you."

My lips moved but nothing came out. I liked the quirky demon but I didn't think I could ever trust him enough to fall in love. He didn't really fit the fire and brimstone that people pictured when they thought mazzikim. I sure as hell didn't represent the ideal succubus. We were a good fit in an odd sort of way. "You have to understand that I'm somewhat emotionally unstable."

"Why can Cooper be a friend with benefits? What makes him so special?"

Ugh, could I get any more nauseous? I rubbed my tummy and scowled at John. "My dad pre-approved him."

His eyebrows rose. "That's quite a requirement."

"Tell me about it." I scowled. "But no one says no to Flynn Blyton when he makes up his mind. He means well. The last time I fell in love it almost killed me."

John spine straightened as if startled. "Your dad rules Lake City."

"I know. What a pain."

He blinked. "You really are going to get me killed." He sounded stunned as well. "My kind doesn't do

121

well with love either." Scratching his head, he eyed me. "So your father preapproves your lovers and Sin makes sure you stick to this roster?"

"It's a long story. In short, Sin was taking care of me since I'm a fuck-up and even with him watching over my shoulder I'm still a mess. My dad's taking over and insists I use—use a small group of males that I'm not going to fall in love with." I still couldn't say the word *suitor* without being drowned in shame.

"So he's interviewing—"

"Potential lovers for me. Yeah." I twiddled with the edge of my sweater. "So, uh, see you around?"

"Yeah, sure." He backed away to let me jump off the counter and escape our uncomfortable discussion.

I took the elevator down to Sin's apartment.

When I exited the elevator, I could hear the swish of his sword cutting through the air at incredible speeds. Every evening when he woke he went through these fighting stances. He said it cleared his mind. I thought he just liked to pretend to kill things since in modern times it was frowned upon to behead your enemy on the streets. I sat on the mat and watched in silence.

He paused and tossed me an annoyed glance. "What?"

"You move well for an old guy." I grinned as his frown grew deeper.

"Why is your eye swollen?" He changed weapons and used two scimitars for this round of exercises. I could almost see him on the battlefield covered in blood and gore. He must have been in heaven in those days.

"Someone stuck their elbow in it by accident."

He knelt in front of me and tilted my head to the side. "It might bruise. Do you want me to kill them?" From most people, I would have laughed at their joke. Sin wasn't part of that group because he wasn't joking. Not even a little bit.

"No. It really was an accident." I hoped. John's kind lived off pain, even the accidental kind. It was an interesting strategy if that's how he fed.

Sin nodded and returned to his weapons exercise.

I sighed and tugged at a loose thread on the practice mat.

He stopped again. "What is it now?"

"Do you know who else my dad has picked?"

"No. Why did I wake with my shoulder smelling like dried tears and snot?"

I jumped, my mouth working but nothing came out.

"Don't tell me, because I really don't want to know. I will not let you twist me in knots no matter how cute you act." He strode to his bathroom.

I undressed and followed Sin into his luxurious shower.

He scrubbed at his shoulder as if trying to take a layer of skin off. "I'm regretting giving you access to my

123

apartment."

I kissed him on the back, between his shoulder blades. I would have needed a stepladder to reach anything higher. "You think I'm cute."

He snorted. "I think you're many things. I'm too much of a gentleman to list them all."

This time I snorted. I rested my head on his back and let my hands wander in front of him. "Thank you for letting me use your shoulder to cry on. I needed it." I stroked his cock. "Turn around?" I bent to my knees as he did as I asked. There was something empowering in sucking cock.

The way Sin's anger melted into heavy-lidded desire by just watching me kneel gave me a much needed surge of confidence. I lapped at his balls, taking one at a time inside my mouth and rolling it with my tongue.

He moaned and rested his back against the shower wall and braced his legs as if needing support to stay on his feet.

I kissed my way along his erection, sipping at the drip of hot water. The skin covering his iron-hard rod brushed my lips like silk. I circled his crown with the tip of my tongue and dipped at the small entrance, tasting the saltiness of his pre-cum.

"Fuck, Pia." He tangled his fingers in my hair. I loved the way he said my name. It was like a combination of curse and plea.

Opening my mouth, I slid him past my lips to the back of my throat and gagged a little on his size. Too much, too fast, but my sister Rose had explained how most males liked the sound. It made them feel big. Sin being an ancient, powerful vampire didn't matter. They all wanted to think they had big dicks.

He thrust, helping me get past the gag and going straight to deep-throating. Such a helpful vampire.

I took him hard, fast, and deep. Not letting him catch his breath.

His hips flexed as he tried to keep up with my pace. A growl rolled in his chest that sounded scarier than any shifter's. Sex between feeds were different. It wasn't about my orgasm for once and I finally got to really focus on my lover. Watching Sin come undone from my attention was epic.

He arched his back, eyes squeezed shut, his lips slack with ecstasy. His seed splashed down my throat as his mouth widened in a silent scream. He finally shuddered and slid down the wall, dragging me down onto his lap. "If you started my evenings like that every day, I might actually start acting nicer."

"Liar."

He kissed my swollen eye. "I'm usually better at sounding honest. I must be slipping." The phone by his bed rang and he heaved a sigh. Setting me aside, he grabbed a towel and answered the call. The pleasant expression on his face fell. "I'm on my way." He motioned at me to join him.

I shut off the water and grabbed a towel. "What is

it?"

"Your father's here and he's pissed."

Chapter Fourteen

"No." I pulled the towel around me tighter. "Tell him I'm out shopping."

The glare Sin tossed me cut as he dressed. "This isn't a negotiation."

"I'm not ready to face him."

He scooped me into his arms and threw me over his shoulder a la caveman, then marched toward the elevator.

"Clothes. Please, please, let me get clothes."

He set me inside the box and let the doors close.

"You ass!" I swung a punch at his shoulder.

With the ease of a well-oiled machine, he stepped out of reach and let me hit the wall.

I clutched my fist. "Ow."

"Don't try to hit me. It's—"

"Pathetic?"

"Detrimental to your health. At my age, my reflexes are quicker than my thought. I'd hurt you." He set

127

my clothes in my hands. I hadn't seen him carrying them.

"Thanks." I raced against the elevator and it won, but at least, I'd covered the important bits with bra and underwear. My father hadn't raised nuns. Didn't mean I wanted to greet him for the first time in months butt naked.

The elevator dinged and the doors slid open.

Neither Sin nor I exited.

The lights flickered as if someone had set off a silent alarm. Distant cries echoed from different directions of the nest. Were we under attack?

I stepped toward Sin and clung to his arm. "I thought you said it was my dad."

"It is. Stay close." His voice shook. "Flynn!" He shouted my father's name.

A tide of bodies rolled out of the main nest's room. They fell to the floor in all manners of undress, tangling in caresses and more intimate acts.

Daddy followed.

Since I couldn't breathe, all the oxygen in the nest seemed to have vanished, or it might be the sight of all the naked people gyrating on the floor. My father stood in the center of the sexual storm dressed in his tailored suit. His skin glowed, not with light, but with sexual power. He had ruled this city for a long time but I had never seen him flex his magical muscles.

Sin's guards, tech and weapons were useless in the face of my father. The vampires, the humans, and the shifters all lay at his feet fucking each other senseless.

I wiggled my fingers at him. "Hi, Daddy." Pride swelled my chest and dread knotted my gut. He didn't send his power toward me and Sin, so that was good, right?

"What happened to your face, baby?" He stepped over the bodies and ran his thumb under my swollen eye. His gaze darted to Sin before his free hand gripped the vampire's throat. "You better not have been playing your rough games with my daughter, little drake."

"It wasn't him, daddy. It was a demon and it was an accident."

Sin didn't need to breathe and breaking his neck wouldn't harm him permanently, but the wooden stake my father pulled out of his jacket would. "We need to talk." He shoved Sin further in the elevator.

Sin rubbed his neck. "What about my people?"

"It will wear off by tomorrow. They'll walk funny for a few days." He gripped the stake in one hand and my arm in the other. "I can't say the same for you though."

"Daddy, let me explain—"

"Oh, I plan on letting you. Your mother came home in tears yesterday and hasn't gotten out of bed since. I'm not leaving this forsaken hole in the ground until I understand why my daughter can't come home. Finish dressing." Once I'd done as he ordered, he motioned for Sin to start the elevator back to the apartment.

My mom wasn't getting out of bed? What had I done? I just kept making things worse. This was why I should stay away from them.

The trip farther underground was as uncomfortable as riding a porcupine butt naked. I stared at my manicured toes the whole way and ignored the staring match next to me. The doors opened into Sin's apartment, where he led us to his private office.

My dad set me on the Italian leather couch by the wall before pacing the office's width. "I'm done playing games." He kept the stake ready in his hand. "You're coming home tonight, Pia." He jabbed his finger toward me.

I jumped. He'd never used that tone of voice with me before. Not even after I poured sugar in Rose's gas tank when she'd stolen my day three feed. I didn't share with my sisters. That was just gross. This version of my father didn't live with us. This version ruled Lake City.

Sin leaned against his desk. "She's mine until the terms of our blood contract are fulfilled."

"The contract says she's yours to take care of, not to keep."

I pulled up my knees to my chest. "But I want to stay."

"Of course you do, but obviously you can't be trusted to make the right decisions." His words stung so hard I couldn't breathe.

Sin reached into a desktop box and pulled out an old-fashioned appearing scroll. He unrolled it, revealing blood script. "Our contract hasn't faded so the terms have not been satisfied. If you break it, then I own your soul." Did he not see the wooden stake in my father's hands? "She's mine to care for until she's well."

"She looks healthy to me."

"Physically, but mentally she's a mess." My gut clenched with Sin's insult. Truth hurt and the vampire wielded it like a club. "Why were you crying on my shoulder this afternoon, Pia?"

"Why are you both doing this? You're hurting me even more." I slammed my fist against the armrests. "Maybe you both need to back off and let me decide what's best for me."

My father pulled out his cell phone. He showed me the picture Sin had sent him from the motel, then swiped it and showed me a picture of me unconscious on Sin's bed after being caned. "Is my point made?"

"I'm allowed to make mistakes." I sagged deeper into the chair. Hadn't I just been thinking about seeing my family again? My dad was changing my mind.

"Not this drastic."

Sin watched with a thoughtful look. "We shouldn't let her use Joshua. I thought him being gentle with women would soothe her heart but I think it might make things worse."

"You mean as one of my suitors?" I perked up. "I like him." He'd been very gentle and receptive of me on my first night in the nest.

131

"Exactly."

Dad scowled. "If not Joshua, then who? I didn't approve anyone else from your nest."

"Me."

My father slammed the stake into Sin's desk, splintering it into the beautiful finished top. "You're not an option."

"According to our contract she's still mine until healthy. I'm willing to re-negotiate for different terms."

I could hear my father grind his teeth. The muscles along his jaw popped with the strain. "Sin." He said the vampire's name as if swearing.

"Zur-Sin." The vampire's voice dropped an octave in his frustration. "Why can't you or your daughter ever address me by my full name?"

Dad coughed. His face relaxed as I glimpsed a smile hidden behind his hand.

Sin's scowl grew deeper. "She won't ever love me and I won't hurt her. Not unless I have a death wish." He eyed the stake protruding from his desk. "It's not like she's at risk of falling in love with me."

"No, but she's at risk of being influenced by you." Dad glanced at me. "What do you think?"

I glared. "Wow, you're actually going to give me a say?" Sarcasm weighted my words. "I won't fall in love with Sin. He's too mean." I wanted Sin. He was the closest thing I'd ever have to a friend, so I stuck out my tongue at him.

He winked in response.

Dad ran his fingers through his short, curly hair. Of all my parents, I resembled him the most, from the crazy hair to bright blue eyes to our penchant of setting the kitchen on fire. "We'll change the terms of the contract then. You'll be one of her suitors but she returns home with me tonight. She's no longer allowed to live in your nest."

"Who's the other suitor you've chosen for me?" I held my breath.

"Lothaire."

I gasped. He was the wolf pack alpha and the biggest womanizer in the city. Heck, he'd slept with both my sisters. The ick factor alone was enough for me to pull the plug on this idea. "No way, never in a million year, no no no." I shook my head. "I won't let him touch me."

"Your sisters recommended him." He sounded genuinely shocked.

I slashed my hand across the air. "No. That's final. I won't feed from Lothaire. Not even if he were the last person on the planet. I'd screw sheep first."

Dad pinched the bridge of his nose. He only did that when he was getting a headache. "I can't interview the whole city, Pia. Do *you* have any suggestions?"

I glanced at Sin.

He curled his lip. He knew who I was thinking of.

"John. He works for Sin on computers." I gave

my father my best smile.

"Pia is forgetting to mention that he's a mazzikim demon," Sin added.

"Yes, but—"

"A *mazzikim* demon."

I sighed. "Yes." I was more familiar with this tone of questioning. This was the lawyer part of my father coming out.

"Who hit you?"

"He did, but by accident with his elbow. He even iced it afterwards." I did my best to sound reasonable. I knew he wouldn't like this idea, but if not John, then who? Sin wouldn't let me have Gigi. I'd have to start suitor shopping in bars or something. "John's a good pick. I couldn't ever trust him enough to fall in love and I don't think his kind *can* love."

"Love is a dangerous thing." My dad's eyes turned sad. "Sin told me what happened with the human boy."

Wishing the couch would swallow me whole, I couldn't hold my father's stare and broke eye contact. I knew Sin had told him about Pierre after the incident at Cleaver. That's the whole reason I had to use suitors, but it didn't mean I was comfortable talking about it yet.

I chewed my bottom lip. "I don't really want to talk about it."

He flexed his fingers, inviting me to take his hand again. "Let's take a trip and go get ice cream."

That I could manage.

Chapter Fifteen

We all had our idiosyncrasies. My father's was his love of ice cream. He believed it cured all aliments. Most of the time he was right; I didn't think the magic would work on broken hearts, though.

I sat in the booth of his favorite parlor. It had a 1950s feel to it, right down to the jukebox and red vinyl seat.

My dad carried two hot fudge sundaes with nuts to our table, handing me one. "I had them supersized." He winked. "I missed dinner and you could use a little more weight."

Poking at the fudgy goodness with my spoon, I did my best to avoid meeting his gaze. I had so many things to say but they all sounded petty and vain inside my head. I took a spoonful to stop my mouth from speaking nonsense, and tasted sawdust.

Dad moaned after his first mouthful. "Nothing like homemade ice cream." He shoveled a few more bites into his mouth before his gaze landed on my still full bowl. Sighing, he scooped another spoonful and held it front of me.

I stared as it dripped on the tabletop. In our culture it was a very old tradition for an incubus to hand feed the succubi he cared for. Not many did it, but old ones, such as my dad, still held to some of the old ways, like the use of suitors. I leaned forward and ate the offered spoonful. "Yours tastes better."

"They're the same kind." Yet he still swapped our bowls. "Eat."

"Yes, Daddy." I took another bite to appease him.

He set his spoon on the table and watched me finish before pushing his bowl in front of me.

"I'm not that starved." I took a spoonful and offered it to him instead. "I'm good."

He looked old all of a sudden. Our people didn't age. Humans around us must have thought us a couple instead of father and daughter but the eyes of our kind changed with what they've seen. My father had seen a lot and it all showed. "I've missed you." He took the spoon and ate the ice cream.

"You're not allowed to make me cry in public. I did enough of that yesterday when I ran into Mom."

His face turned grim. "I promised everyone I'd drag you home kicking and screaming if I had to. You're not going to make me do that, are you?"

I gazed into the bowl of melting cream and swirled chocolate as if a vision of my future lay in there. It was so muddled and cloudy it may as well have been. "I don't want to go home. I like it in Sin's nest."

He reached across the table, resting his hand on

mine. "What happened, Pia?"

"You said Sin told you." I recalled those sunny days with Pierre when I had pretended to be human, and they were sadly the happiest days of my life.

"He told me of the boy, but I know that's not the whole story. You wouldn't have tried to kill yourself over falling in love with a human. It wouldn't have driven you away from *us*."

My stomach cramped. I leaned away from the table and my father.

He got up and came to my side, scooting me over on the bench so we sat shoulder to shoulder. "Did I ever tell you about when I first came to America?"

"Yes." It had been during the Great Famine in 1847. Things had been bad in Europe. When humans suffered, so did we since they were the root of our food source.

"I was young for an incubus to be on his own with no wives to feed from. I was lonely too." He rested his arm over my shoulders and pulled me against him. "I met this pretty human girl. She was alone too. Her family had perished from the flu, on the journey across the ocean." He sighed. "I loved her so much."

I twisted in my seat to face him. "She couldn't feed you."

He shook his head. "No and I couldn't be faithful like she deserved. In the end I broke her heart and mine as well. My point is that we aren't made to be in relationships with other races."

I leaned my head against him, knowing this could be the last time my dad would ever hold me again, and was tempted to pretend the source of my conflict was just a broken heart. How long before I wouldn't be able to face my own reflection in the mirror, though? Eventually someone would find out what I'd done and word would get to my family. Lying would only make it worse. "I fed from a married man," I whispered, hoping he heard me and wouldn't make me repeat it.

From the way his shoulders went tense I knew he heard me clearly. "Well, that's unfortunate." He shifted in his seat. "Sin didn't mention that."

"He doesn't understand our ways." I slipped out from under my dad's arms and waited for him to leave. Succubi who broke up marriages were usually shunned by our people. Marriage was the base of our society. Without it, we would return to the savage days when incubi hunted us like animals.

"No, he doesn't. Neither do you." He pulled me against him in a fierce hug that drew questioning looks. My bones creaked but I stayed silent. "By all the gods old and new, you will put me in an early grave. Did you do it on purpose?"

"No, I was starved. I lost control."

"It was a stupid move to feed just from the boy."

"Pierre."

He pulled away and gave me a stare.

"He has a name. I wish I could forget him, but I

can't. He's here." I pointed at my heart. "Hopefully not forever. You right, I was stupid. I can't help how I feel, though."

"No, I think you get that from me as well. I always fell in love so easily."

"So you think this suitor idea will make it easier for me?"

"For a while. I don't think it's a permanent thing. Just until you can trust your judgment again." He smirked. "Or until *I* can trust your judgment again to not think you can feed off one person for the rest of your life."

I nodded.

"Let's go home, Pia. Your mothers and sisters have been worried sick about you for months. You can't leave them like that. After your visit, if you still insist on returning to Sin I'll drive you there myself."

A huge weight lifted off my shoulders. I feared I would float off the bench, but my father anchored me because that's what family was for. No matter how much of a jackass I was, they still loved me. Warmth welled inside my chest and filled the emptiness that had been plaguing me for months. "Okay."

Epilogue

Day three of my cycle

Sin rolled off of me, licking his lips clean of my blood. His skin was slick with sweat. "Where did you learn that trick?" He breathed heavily.

A smug smile pulled at my lips. I'd never heard him shout as he came before. I'd have to thank my sister Adele for teaching me how to twist my hips like that. It seemed like even old vampires didn't know everything. I stretched. "Ancient succubus secret."

"Your father hasn't set fire to my nest so I assume all is well on your home front."

"All unpacked and back at home where I belong." I rolled into his arms and took advantage of his satisfied state to steal some snuggle time. I might not have the kind of loving relationship most people had, but I got what I needed emotionally from my three suitors. "Do you miss me?"

"It's quieter."

"Admit it. You're bored now that I'm gone." Happiness had seemed so unattainable a few months ago but like a ninja it had snuck up on me.

He grinned. "I have other hobbies to keep me

occupied. Speaking of which, while I was on my business trip I encountered someone I'd like you to meet."

"Why? I have enough suitors."

"He's an incubus."

"I can't feed from incubi. It's the other way around."

Sin growled. "I know that."

"Then why would you want me to meet an incubus? Did my father put you up to this? I'm not interested in a cold, loveless marriage." I was still starved for love though. We lived a long time so I hoped one day I'd run across Mr. Right.

He chortled. "I understand that. I was just tossing the idea out there."

"No."

"He seemed…lonely."

"No."

He gave me a devious look.

"If you ever want to experience that thing I did with my hips again, you'll drop the subject."

His lips twitched, but he didn't say another word.

Starved for Love

Book Two, Boys of Lake City

I'm a succubus with an eating disorder that has nothing to do with food. Every three days, I'm have to feed from a different lover.

The most eligible incubus in the country has arrived in Lake City to find a wife. Succubi are flocking to my city for a chance to apply. Even my two gorgeous, confident, and intelligent sisters have appointments to meet him.

Not me.

I'm considered too unstable for marriage. A succubus who wants love? Even my charm won't come close to me incase its contagious.

If only somebody had bothered to tell me to stay away from the Roxy hotel. If only a certain vampire *cough* Sin *cough* hadn't sent me on an errand to said hotel. If only I had paid attention to gossip. Then maybe we wouldn't have met.

Now he wants me.

The crazy sister.

Sinful Cravings

Book Three, Boys of Lake City

I'm a succubus with an eating disorder that has nothing to do with food. Every three days, I'm have to feed from a different lover.

When I don't feed every three days, my demon nature takes over and goes on the hunt. Incubi don't live by those rules. They're always hungry and they can only feed from my kind.

Valerio Hunan is the most eligible incubus in the country and he's taken me as his fiancé. Because of this action, his family has cut him off from his source of succubus energy, and now, I'm on the top of his menu.

Val's demon side makes mine look like a saint. Every time I feed him, I then have to feed myself. And on and on we go until I die. Or we figure out why his other sources of energy have stopped their shipments.

Starved for Love

Chapter One

Day three of my cycle

Sex and love should come in the same package, but for a succubus, that meant trouble. Sex equaled food and fidelity couldn't be part of the equation. Humans couldn't eat the same thing every meal and stay healthy, and neither could we.

I thumped on the steel door of an industrial garage. Most people didn't know the largest vampire nest in the Northeast was contained in an underground facility below this building. I kept up my third round of pounding. I knew the vampires were in there. The sun had just set. Someone needed to drag his lazy butt out of bed to answer the door. "I'm not going away!" Security cameras and microphones monitored the place 24/7. The jerks knew I was here.

I needed to feed, and to do that, I needed to get laid. Like all succubi, I survived on the energy created in my body during an orgasm. I couldn't even stay alive on bad sex. Finding attractive, skilled partners wasn't a problem in Lake City, but I was a sucker for falling in love. I couldn't handle the guilt of a one-night stand, and if I tried to live off one male forever, I'd starve, which my instincts wouldn't allow. I'd tried it once and would never allow myself to go down that road again.

Neither would my parents.

Rain plastered my short curls to my head. Normally, they stuck straight out, the different shades of autumn leaves. I'd be lucky if my suitor didn't slam the door in my face at the sight of my drenched appearance. But I needed him in a bad way.

I added a kick to my knocking. "It's Pia, damn it. And it's raining. Let me in."

The door finally opened. "The Master's not expecting you for another seven days."

I pushed past Rat, one of Zur-Sin's minions, and huddled in the antechamber. "I know. Tell him I have a problem."

"What trouble are you in now, Pia?" Sin's voice carried over an intercom by the door leading into the vampire lair.

Pressing the talk button, I stood on tiptoe to speak in the microphone. "John left a note pinned to my door. He left town last night." I hoped he was okay. Being a low-level demon bites. Someone was always on his ass.

"So?"

"He's my suitor for today." I glanced at Rat, who chuckled. "Shut up."

"Go see Cooper."

"Cooper's on a hunting trip with the pack. Won't be back for another three days when it's his turn."

"I can oblige." Rat stroked a hand down my back.

His touch sent a wave of desire through my body, but I wasn't so far gone yet that I'd jump anything with a dick. "Fuck off." I shoved him away. At least, I tried to. Beauty was a succubus power, not muscle. "We made a deal, Sin."

"Every nine days. You were just here three days ago."

"Yeah, do the math, genius. Today's day three in my cycle. You want me to do Rat instead? I'm out of options." I crossed my arms and glared at the vampire lackey. I'd eat my own arm before touching him but Sin didn't have to know that.

"Bring her down, Ratan."

Rat's fanged grin faded. "Yes, Master." He unlocked the door and opened it for me like a gentleman. "Whores first."

I pulled my jacket tighter around me and fought the shivers. Half-drowned, my need burned inside my body, the hunger for flesh rubbing on flesh setting my skin to oversensitive. If Sin didn't take me to his bed then I'd have to find some stranger to screw. Nausea rolled in my stomach. I never should have been born a succubus. To my parent's shame and concern, I wasn't amoral enough.

They monitored my every meal. How much worse could my life get when my father interviewed potential lovers for me? For crying out loud, what happened with Pierre was history and they needed to let go of the past. I did. Tried…

Racing down the stairs and across the sub-basement, I strode by other vampires, all of them part of Zur-Sin's nest. He controlled Lake City at night and my father had it during the day. That's how I met Sin. My father hooked me up about five years ago to keep me from starving.

Twenty-five years old and I still lived with my parents. All four of them.

Most mortals wouldn't understand my dad being interested in my sex life, but he worried and stressed about my lack of lovers to feed upon since I was so picky. I had three now. That should be more than enough if they would just cooperate.

I waited for Rat to twist his key in the elevator so it would travel into the secured areas below us. The doors slid open and I jumped inside.

"Try not to take too long. He has appointments to keep." With those lovely instructions, Rat keyed the doors closed and I descended into Sin's world.

Shaking the excess water from my hair, I tried to poof some life back into my signature curls. They sagged on my forehead. Sighing at my reflection, I hung my head. Nothing was sadder than a disheveled, horny succubus.

The doors slid open and a large pair of bare feet stepped into my view. A finger slipped under my chin and raised my gaze. Zur-Sin, ancient vampire warrior, stared at me with his stern dark eyes. Dressed in only a pair of black silk pajama bottoms, he looked good enough to eat. He brushed the curls from my face and frowned. "You have much to learn about the art of seduction."

"I dressed up last time I was here. I get panicky when things don't go my way on day threes."

"It's not all about appearance, Pia. You're beautiful even when left out in the rain." He bent and placed a gentle kiss on my lips. Sin's touch always struck a spark— even on my off days he could lure me to his bed. "Grace and tact would be appreciated at times. You can't barge into my nest making demands. It makes me seem weak."

"I'm sorry." I leaned against his solid chest. His pale skin still retained the warmth of his last feed. I didn't ask about his latest conquest. We had a business deal signed in blood. He gave me an orgasm every nine days and I fed him with my blood. No strings attached. I think I came out on top of that deal because Sin could be a generous

147

lover when in the right mood. And I had learned how to guide him into those moods.

He placed a kiss to the top of my head. "Next time call. I have a human secretary, remember? She'd have made quieter arrangements."

"She hates me." I squirmed, pressing my thighs together to help relieve the growing demands between them.

Sin sighed and led me into his apartment, through the living room, past his office and into the bedroom where he sat on the edge of his king-sized bed. He plucked a remote off the mattress and turned on some slow jazz. Leaning back onto his elbows, he ran his gaze over me. "Undress."

I knew this game. It was his favorite. The command was a comfort, something familiar in a day filled with anxiety, since my scheduled suitor had abandoned me. I had watched the sun move across the sky, feeling my need grow. Unbuttoning my raincoat, I tossed it to the floor. I listened to the music and allowed the beat to pace my movements. Shirt, jeans and socks came off slow and easy. Each stroke of my hand over my skin intensified my yearning.

All the while he watched, his eyes caressing my curves, so intent it made me ache.

I unclasped the front of my bra and stalked toward the edge of the bed. The straps slid from my shoulders and down my arms, releasing my breasts. Cool air brushed over my wet skin and sent a shiver through my limbs.

"You're cold." He offered me his hand.

I climbed in his warm bed. Lying next to him, I ran my hand through his short, sunny-blond hair. "What would I do without you?"

He chuckled. "Save those words for your other

suitors." Trailing a sharp fingernail over my breastbone, he drew a path to my belly button and teased the small ring pierced there. "What will you give me in exchange for tonight?"

I blinked and tilted my head to see his face better. "What I always pay, my blood."

He shook his head. "I already fed and the price went up."

"Sin."

"Zur-Sin." His dark gaze pinned me to the spot. Sometimes I forgot how old he truly was. The young-looking man lying next to me wasn't from my generation and could be crueler than Lucifer when he wanted to be.

I swallowed the cold lump of fear in my throat. "What do you want?"

Bending over my nipple, he circled it with the tip of his tongue.

I groaned and arched toward his devilish mouth, unable to control my traitorous body.

Every three terrible days, I had to have an orgasm. My body wouldn't stop until I did or I died. The more the need grew, the less control I had, until I was humping some poor schmuck in an alley. May that never, ever, happen again.

"A business rival of mine is in town. Valerio Hunan. I hear rumors he's thinking of staying. I need to know if he is and what his plans are." He blew over the wet spot he'd created. It sent a sharp pang of desire straight to my core. "You can practice your grace and tact on him and then tell me what I want to know." He rolled on top of me, pinning my hands to the bed.

"I'm terrible at espionage. Ask my father." I writhed under Sin. Not because I wanted escape, but to rub against his fine muscled body. The vampire was built to kill.

He settled between my willing thighs and rocked. "Time to grow up, Pia."

"You're such a tease." I flung my head back in frustration. "Fine. Sex first."

He chuckled, dark and deep; the sound made my soul tremble. "Of course." With his sharp nail, he scratched the inside of my wrist.

I twisted to look at our hands. "What are you doing?"

"This pact has to be sealed in blood." He did the same to his wrist—

"Wait…"

—and pressed our wounds together.

"Shit, Sin." I yanked my hand away. "You can be such an ass." If I broke a deal sealed in blood, he'd never help me again. I hated to admit it but Sin was my go-to guy for almost everything.

"You didn't think I've obtained my position on charm and good looks?" He leaned toward his bedside table and buzzed his intercom.

"Yes, Master?"

"Reschedule my appointments. I'll be busy for the rest of the night." He flipped it off, knelt between my legs and, with practiced ease, slithered out of his bottoms. Trailing his fingers over my damp panties, he finally smiled, exposing his deadly fangs. "Let's make sure you're well fed."

I wanted to kick him in the balls but the last time I tried such a dumbass move he'd spanked me. Hard. I couldn't sit for a week.

Hooking a finger under my panties, he dragged them off my hips until I lay bare under him. "Where should we start this time?" He nipped at my collarbone as he ran his hands along my torso and hips.

"Sin." His name dragged out of my throat. In a flash of desire my anger went poof. I'd find it tomorrow, tossed behind the bone-melting satisfaction he'd leave me in, and probably be too exhausted to care.

He swept his fingers between my folds. "Always so wet for me, Pia." With familiar aim, he pinched my clit, rolling it between his fingertips.

"Oh shit." I thrust my hips, raising them off the mattress. No matter what, I'd always be putty in his hands. A toy, a tool in a moment of his long existence, and I never doubted that he would outlive us all.

Guiding my legs over his shoulders, he bent me in half as he pressed the tip of his cock against my entrance. "Say it."

I bit the bottom of my lip as I met his gaze.

Rocking his hips, he cock teased, driving just inside of me, then withdrawing. "I can do this all night."

I knew he could—the bastard had done it before. He'd left me a quivering mass by morning. Sometimes I hated him. He'd make me say it.

He continued to stroke me in all the right places until I panted, the need so strong I thought it would burn me from the inside out.

"Please."

"Please, what?"

"Master," I cried out. As soon as the word left my lips, he plunged inside of me to the hilt.

Hard and fast, he pumped with my ankles around his neck. Like everything Sin did, he pushed with power and confidence.

I met every stroke, squeezed him with my secret muscles and felt every inch of his length. My need loved the energy he helped create.

It was dark and potent, curling inside my belly, then lashing out in a burst of adrenaline. What we created together carried an edge to it like suicidally hot wings. I loved their spiciness, but they were cruel to me, just like him. Nothing would keep me from ordering them, though. Sin was my zesty suitor, setting all my succubus taste buds on fire.

My body had the capacity to create energy from sex, but my partners each added a mysterious element of themselves that helped sate my need. That's why masturbation didn't work. I needed that pinch of sexual oomph from a lover to make my motor roar.

Each thrust brought me closer to the edge until I finally stepped off, crying his name until I was hoarse. Heat swelled in my abdomen as his seed spilled into me. The warmth spread as my body generated the added nourishment I needed to survive.

Millions of years of evolution, descended from demons, and yet we were still parasites, living off other species, slaves to their sexual desires so we could survive.

Sin released his hold and rolled off me.

Groping for my purse on the floor by the bed, I searched inside for a glass vial. The cork popped off easily and I pressed the edge against my lips. A slow spill of blue energy poured inside until the bottle filled, then I capped it.

Sin watched with mild interest. "Do your sisters still feed your father as well?"

"Yes." I set the vial in my purse. An incubus could only feed from a succubus and most incubi kept a harem of wives. But our mothers couldn't support our father's growing needs. The stronger the incubus, the more he fed, and my dad co-ruled a city. He should be shopping for a new wife, but oddly for our people, he loved our mothers so much he feared breaking the delicate balance they enjoyed.

Fidelity didn't fit in our lifestyle. Since my sisters and I were old enough to feed, we decided to do our part by placing a small portion of our feeds in vials. This was only a patch, not a solution. Governing the charm, a group of succubi and incubi, in Lake City took power, but our supplemental feedings sustained him for now.

"That's sweet." Sin's tone didn't reflect his words.

"What is up your ass tonight?" I picked up my panties only to have him swipe them from my hand.

"You need to find more suitors. The three you have aren't enough." He yanked me back into his arms.

"I've learned my lesson. I promise to never barge into here again." I turned away and faced the wall.

"That's not the point, Pia. You have to embrace your nature. Your sisters don't have suitors. They—"

"Fuck around. I get it. I should be a slut."

He rested his forehead against my shoulder. "What if I wasn't here today? What if you had to make do with Rat?"

I closed my eyes, trying not to picture that image. "I don't know."

153

"You need backup. Would a mortal once in a while be so bad?"

"Did my father ask you to have this talk with me?"

He laughed and it sounded easier and lighter than before. "No, but contrary to popular belief, I do care about what happens to you." He pressed a kiss against the back of my neck, his hand tracking toward my breast. "Think about it."

I rolled onto my back and wrapped my arms around his neck. "I think you owe me a night of pleasure, Master." I knew Sin cared but his brand of fuzzies stung.

He opened the drawer by the bed. "Let's see what kind of toys I left in here."

www.ingramcontent.com/pod-product-compliance
Lightning Source LLC
Chambersburg PA
CBHW022129150726
47992CB00002B/514